LET THE CHURCH SAY

KINYEL FRIDAY

Published by

KinYori Books, LLC

46036 Michigan Avenue, #283

Canton, MI 48188

www.KinyelFriday.com

Let the Church Say © 2024. All rights reserved. No part of this book may be reproduced or used in any manner, including electronic, mechanical, or photocopying, or stored in a retrieval system without the express written permission of the publisher, except for the use of brief quotations in a book review.

ISBN 979-8-9916887-0-3

Cover Illustration: Robert Roberson, Jr.

Illustration Copyright © 2024

Manufactured and printed in the United States of America

This book is a work of fiction. Characters, events, and incidents are the product of the author's imagination. The author uses a few names of actual places as a point of reference. Any resemblance of actual persons, living or dead, or events is purely coincidental. This book contains language that may be considered profane or offensive to some readers. Reader discretion is advised.

Contents

Introduction v
The Thickest Blood 1
Picnic Ants 21
Is This the End? 41
Mousetrap 65
Still Waters 81
Silver Bells 95
You Never Know 111
A Season 139
Epilogue 153

Introduction

This book has been a long time coming. I began this journey in 2002, while I was an undergrad, with "The Thickest Blood" as a standalone short story. When I went back to school to earn my master's in English specializing in creative writing, I pulled this out, added to it, and by the time my thesis came around, I submitted six solid stories. Within the last few years, I added two more stories to bring the main character, Hattie Mae Atkins, to a more defined conclusion.

With that being said, each chapter is a single short story that moves chronologically with the same characters. My prayer is that you find the same humor and love I did in this story.

Much love,
Kinyel

The Thickest Blood

Be imitators of God as dearly loved children and live a life of love, just as Christ loved us and gave himself up for us. (Ephesians 5:1 & 2)

"Hey, Mama. Where are you?"

Hattie closed her thickened Bible, full of turned down pages and scraps of paper saturated with notes and scriptures, and placed it on the end table next to her.

"In here, Isaiah." Thunderous steps rushed toward her. *He better not track mud all across my floor and new rug, I know that much.* "Take off your shoes before you come any further. If you track mud all on my floor—"

Isaiah cut her short. "I know, I know. You'll make me get down on my hands and knees and wash the whole floor."

She nodded. Isaiah had had his mother's preachings memorized since he was nine. Thirty years later, she still hadn't changed a bit. He stood in the doorframe and shook his head at her; happy because he loved his mother, but he would be even happier if she found another hobby besides lecturing him every time he stopped by.

"So, what needs to be done today?"

"Look around and pick your startin' place. Nothing really in particular."

Isaiah turned. "Well, then I'm 'bout to go back home."

"No you ain't either! You better find somethin' in here to fix! What about my dishwasher?"

"Did that last week."

"Washing machine?"

"Last month."

"I've got it—how 'bout my truck?"

"What truck?"

"The one in the garage. What other truck would I be talking 'bout?"

"Mama, that truck hasn't been running since I was five years old. I don't even know why you still have it. Plus, you don't even drive no more!"

"Well then get the gettin'! That truck is special to me."

"It's garbage."

"Your father bought it for me, you know."

"And they lasted 'bout the same amount of time, too."

She got hot. "Don't you talk about your daddy! Don't you say another word!" Tears welled up in her eyes. Isaiah backed down. He didn't want to upset her any further and raise her blood pressure. Isaiah just didn't understand why she held on to that rusty old piece of junk—or his memory. He reluctantly agreed to look at the truck and went out to the garage.

*   *   *

Hattie Mae Atkins and Benjamin Baker were married on February 21, 1968, in Jackson, Mississippi. Isaiah was born a year later, and in four more, they welcomed their baby girl, Ruth Anne. The couple struggled to keep money in the house, food on the table, and their love strong, although the latter was only a struggle for Benjamin.

Wild Cat, as Hattie sometimes called her husband due to his adventurous nature, left her while she was dropping their sick two-month-old at her mother-in-law's and Isaiah at preschool on her way to work. Dinner was cold as ice after sitting on Wild Cat's placemat from six that night to eight the next morning. She called his friend Sammy at the police station several times and asked him to look for Benjamin, but never received a call back. Hattie continued making dinner plates for her ghost of a husband until a week later when she saw him walking arm in arm with a woman across the street who looked as if she were barely out of junior high school. Just laughing it up, while his hand was stationed on her swollen belly. Hattie and the kids were all bundled up for a windy yet routine trip to the corner grocery store. With his eyes half covered by his royal blue hood, an excited Isaiah called out to him, but Benjamin ignored his cries and kept on walking. Didn't even bother to acknowledge his own child's existence. Hattie guessed either Sammy didn't want to deliver the bad news or he flat out hadn't looked. This became Hattie's wake-up call and the birth of a saved Christian woman.

Heartbroken and humiliated, Hattie Mae packed up a U-Haul and moved to Michigan to be near one of her best friends from school, Bea, while dropping her married name and picking up a newfound faith in God. She still loved Wild Cat, though she hated herself for it. Hattie just couldn't bring herself to draw up the papers to permanently sever the ties. She didn't believe in divorce and instead threw herself at the mercy of the church in hopes that time would heal her.

* * *

Hattie's first church service was a memorable one. She was ashamed that the last time she'd set foot in a sanctuary, she was eleven, although she'd passively wished for a closer relationship with God over the years. Hattie slowly walked into Faithful God, Our Heavenly Savior & Glory Methodist Church gripping her son's hand at her side and cradling her daughter's tiny body securely to her chest. She nervously looked around and muttered "Good morning" to all of the smiling faces that passed by and spoke to her.

She sat quietly in the second to last pew, even when the pastor asked if there were any newcomers. By the time it came to testify, Hattie couldn't hold back any longer. Her heart was too heavy. She started crying like a newborn baby, bringing unwanted attention to herself. A woman who was sharing her sad story a couple of rows in front of her stopped talking to look at Hattie for a moment.

"Sister, I think you need this more than I do. Go on and testify. He listens." The church roared with encouragement, then applauded when Hattie finally rose from her seat.

Hattie's hands shook as she looked around the congregation at thirty pairs of eyes patiently awaiting her story. "I," her voice trailed off. She swallowed hard.

"Take your time," a member shouted.

She wiped her sweaty brow with the back of her hand and brushed the wetness off onto her skirt. "I just moved here with my two kids and, and—I can't do this." She plopped back down embarrassed, with her head hanging.

The pastor spoke into his microphone. "We all are family here. There's nothing to be ashamed or afraid of. John chapter one, verse nine says that 'If we confess our sins, He is faithful and just and will forgive us our sins and purify us from all unrighteousness.'"

A heap of "amens," "Hallelujahs," and "Praise Hims" echoed off of the matchbox-like church as if they were cued. Hattie took another look around at all the people who were staring at her. *That's why they call it a family. There's only a handful of people in here. Everybody knows your business!*

Hattie stood up again and cleared her throat uneasily. "Well, like I said, I just moved here—from Mississippi. And, this is Ruth Anne and Isaiah," she said as she lifted her daughter and brought Isaiah to his feet, holding his chilly hand. "I'm Hattie. Hattie Mae Atkins. We're new to the city. I've got one friend here, but no family." Hattie allowed the tears to fall.

The pastor outstretched his arms and confidently stated, "You do now." The congregation shouted more praises to Him, welcomed them, and started into a ten-minute song that was meant to be only three minutes, tops. It was uplifting to Hattie, but not for Isaiah, who kept squirming around in his Sunday's best on the hard pew. The songs, sermon, and scriptures all moved Hattie like never before. She felt as if they were all directed to her, like she was destined to be there. After church, Hattie stopped at the first bookstore to buy her very own Bible, then went home to study.

*   *   *

Hattie dried her eyes and sat in her favorite chair, staring off into space. She loosened the cloth belt around her dress; she felt uncomfortable. After Benjamin left her, she added an easy forty-five pounds to her once slightly curvy figure. Now, five-foot-nine, 366 pounds, she realized she couldn't blame all of her extra meat on her estranged husband. It was all the church bake sales, banquets, breakfasts before church, and the list went on. Hattie never missed a meal, and her church family encouraged her to cook for every event. Her cooking was so good that the activities director added some extra cookout days into the calendar and told his wife to work next to Hattie and take notes.

Hattie struggled to her feet and wobbled to the bathroom. Each day was getting harder and harder, like she wasn't used to all the weight that she had been carrying for years. As soon as she pulled down her girdle, stockings, and BADs (Big-Ass Drawers) to sit, the phone rang. Grateful that she hadn't sat down yet, she pulled her girdle and underwear back up and shuffled to the phone with her stockings cradling her ankles. *This better be good.*

"Hello," she answered curtly.

"Hello. You have a collect call from a resident at Winston Peter Hall Juvenile Detention Center. The resident is '*Your grandson*.' If you accept the charges, please press one; otherwise, please hang up now and no charges will be billed."

Hattie almost dropped the phone. *I never got the chance to meet my grandson. What made him call me of all people? Why is he in a detention center? Isn't that a prison? Oh Lord, what happened to Ruth Anne? Where's my baby?* She picked up her Bible and clutched it tightly to her chest. Hesitantly, she pressed one.

She was greeted with uncomfortable silence. Sure they were flesh and blood, but what do you say to someone you've never met? Where do you start with someone who was only in your dreams and purposefully removed from your life? Hattie Mae and Ruth Anne had been estranged for eighteen years. So a formal meeting of her grandchild was never on the schedule. Hattie would never forget the last time she saw her seventeen-year-old baby girl.

* * *

"C'mon, Ruth Anne. Ain't you dressed yet?" Hattie hollered down the hall. The rest of the family was prepared to leave for Easter dinner at one of their church member's houses, but Ruth Anne was slowing everybody down, as if they weren't already twelve minutes late.

"I hate it when you call me that!" Ruth Anne called from behind the closed door to her room. They'd had this conversation a million times. Ruth Anne preferred to be called Lisa, her middle name. She thought that "Ruth Anne" sounded like a down-home country type of name. She was a city girl who didn't care where her roots were from.

"Do you realize the privilege of being named after such a strong woman? A Biblical woman. An ancestor of the Lord Jesus Christ our Savior? Ruth, chapter one, verse—"

"I know, I know, I know! How many times are you going to preach to me the same stuff over and over again?"

"Until it sinks in." Ever since Ruth Anne had entered Greenfield High and started hanging out with a shady group of girls, she hadn't been the easiest person to deal with. She hadn't applied herself like she should. She wore boyish clothing, ignored curfew, and tried to talk her way out of a few church services due to being out late the night before, but her mother wouldn't have it. Even when Hattie put Ruth Anne in her place, she would go around her friends and get brainwashed all over again.

Ruth Anne walked out from the back room and stood five feet away from her mother. Her long, thick, coarse hair was propped up in a neat ponytail that hung down and kissed the top of her shoulders. Hattie's mouth dropped when she looked her daughter up and down, at her gold loosely fitted jogging suit. Her smug smile made Hattie want to slap her.

"Where you finna go like that? Why aren't you dressed?"

Ruth Anne looked down at herself and commented, "I am dressed. See Mama, these are clothes too." She struck a pose.

Her mother threw her balled up fists on her hips. She had had enough of her smart mouth. "Why don't you have your church clothes on? You took all that time to put on some raggedy jogging suit?"

"I don't have any dresses that can fit. And this ain't raggedy," she retorted, rolling her big brown eyes that were identical to her mother's.

"You didn't try."

"Would you like to?"

Hattie huffed. She took a step closer to Ruth Anne, and Ruth Anne took a step back on the sly. "Go put on that pink dress with the flowers on it."

"It don't fit."

"What about the navy and red one?"

"It don't fit."

"Why? I know you've been eating a whole lotta my gravy and sweet potato pie, but you couldn't have gained twenty pounds overnight." Her mother wore a puzzled look.

"Almost ten so far," she mumbled.

"Whatchu say?" Silence. "What's going on with you? Actin' all crazy and such."

"I'm pregnant," Ruth Anne blurted out. She immediately lowered her eyes and backed up a few feet, afraid her mother might swing.

Hattie's eyes inflated like a balloon. "Oh, sweet Jesus!" was all that she could manage, as her eyes moistened. She raised her arms to the ceiling and continued to call out to Jesus as she sunk down to the floor. Ruth Anne followed. She sat on her legs and allowed the tears to pour. Already four months along, she was relieved that she had finally bared her soul to her mother.

Isaiah kneeled next to his mother and held onto her shaking body, despite her screams and cries. "Lord, please give me strength! I can't take it no mo!"

After fifteen more minutes of this somber scene, no one had bothered to comfort Ruth Anne yet. She was still seated a few feet away, leaning up against the hallway's doorframe, refusing to wipe her tear-stained face. Her "I'm sorrys" went unnoticed by her mother's wailing.

Hattie finally spoke to her daughter. "So when's the wedding?"

Ruth Anne mumbled, "Never, we broke up," as fresh tears wet her face.

Hattie paused. She hadn't even looked at her own daughter since the argument about her clothes. "Well chile, I don't know what else to do with you. I can't have you and some chile out of wedlock layin' up under me, burdening my soul, dragging me straight to Hell along with you. You have committed the *ultimate* sin."

"No, Mama. No." Ruth Anne pleaded. She crawled over to her mother to try and hug her, but Hattie smacked her damp face. Ruth Anne covered the sting and forced out a reply. "Everybody sins, Mama! You can't just—"

"Hush your mouth!" Hattie cut into her. "I don't want to hear another word. You're in God's hands now, not mine. I made up my mind and I want you out of here. Seventeen years just *wasted*! I ain't gonna have this type of foolishness in my house. I *have* no daughter. How dare you embarrass me and yourself before God and our church family."

"I don't care about them! They—"

"Hush up, chile!" Hattie got up, holding her head. She calmly stated her last words to her daughter. "There's no need to argue with me. I told you I made up my mind and that's all there is to it. You've gone way too far for me to try and bring you back now. I want you out! Isaiah, call Sis Bea and tell her somethin' came up. I'm gonna go lie down and I don't want to hear a peep from nobody till the mornin'." Hattie waddled up the creaky steps to her room and slammed her bedroom door shut.

Isaiah scooted over to his sister's defeated body. He held her tight as he lovingly stroked her head. They rocked together in silence.

"You don't think she—" Ruth Anne stuttered.

"Shh. It's okay. She don't mean it, LeeLee. She's just talking. You know how she is."

She sniffed. "Yeah, she's getting crazier and crazier by the minute." They shared a laugh.

At the end of the week, from the kitchen window, Hattie watched her children load Ruth Anne's two overstuffed suitcases and book bag into Isaiah's car. He was ordered to drop his sister off at the Fae Stephens Center, which housed at-risk children from infants to teens, and in a separate building, unwed mothers. Hattie had signed all the necessary paperwork a few days before, so now Ruth Anne officially belonged to Fae Stephens.

Hattie used food to comfort herself and to mask the depression she was feeling in the first month of Ruth Anne's absence, easily gaining fifteen pounds. She would never fess up to being depressed because she thought it meant that she was losing her faith in God. Isaiah was all she had left, and he moved out within the week. Was it her? Why was abandonment becoming such a theme in her life?

* * *

"What's your name, son?" Hattie asked, ashamed that she didn't know her only grandson's name.

"Chris. Christopher Atkins, ma'am."

"What can I do for you, Christopher?"

"I'm being released Friday morning, and I was just wondering if you could come get me."

"Where is this Winston Peter place?"

"Virginia."

"Virginia! Boy, do you know where you called?"

"Um."

"Michigan, boy!" The butterflies in her stomach eased. "What on earth did you do?"

"I stole a car."

"What for?"

"I needed a ride."

Hattie sucked her teeth in total disgust. "Oh my Lord. Where is your mother? You don't have anybody closer who could come get you?"

"Mama said that she was sick of me. Sick of me being bad, or whatever, and just basically disowned me. Actually, I think she changed her number. And, I can't find my auntie who I used to stay with, so I called you."

Hattie's mind drifted off after Christopher said "disowned me." She always prayed that if she ever had an opportunity to get back in touch with her daughter, she would do right. Hattie saw this as her only chance. She wasn't ready to lose another relative. "I'll come get you, baby." They talked for a few more minutes before disconnecting. She found out that Christopher was seventeen. He loved to read, play basketball, and listen to hip hop and jazz. Hattie was taken aback by the jazz, but she was indeed impressed.

"Guess who just called, Isaiah," an excited Hattie shouted, as soon as he put his toe in the door.

"Who?"

"My grandson and your nephew." The only noise from his direction was the door slamming shut. "Boy, do you hear me talking to you?"

Isaiah walked up and leaned against the doorframe separating the living room from the family room. "I hear ya. So what's going on?"

"Well, his name is Christopher. Very polite, for the most part. But he *is* missing some sense."

He shot her a puzzled look. "Whatchu talkin' 'bout, Mama?"

"He's in some detention center or whatever, and—" she started.

Isaiah's eyes grew wide. "He's in juvie? What did he call here for? Where's LeeLee?"

"Ruth Anne turned her back on him, and he needs somebody to pick him up. I can't turn my back on him too. He's got nowhere else to go."

"Why not? You've had plenty of practice cutting family off."

Hattie jumped up from her seat, or at least tried to, but only got to the edge. "Boy, you betta watch your mouth! You ain't too old for me to take my belt to your butt! Don't you think I feel bad enough about losing your sister? I've tried to call her here and there, but she wouldn't accept any of my calls. Then she moved to God only knows where.

"If I could do it all over again, I would've accepted her and her child, but I let my pride get in the way. I was being so selfish thinking that Ruth Anne was trying to embarrass me on purpose. I beg for forgiveness every time I lie and tell everyone who asks about her that she ran away. You've heard me. This is my last chance, Isaiah. All that praying paid off. I told you God is good!"

"Where are you going, who are you going with, and how are you getting there?"

Hattie made her way to the refrigerator while humming Andre Crouch's "The Lord is My Light." "Virginia, you, and you," she answered sequentially.

"Virginia? You crazy. I can't go way down there."

"Why? You got a record too?"

"I don't have any more sick days. And I'm not about to get fired for some knucklehead boy. *And* another thing."

"What's that?"

"You ain't going either."

* * *

Thursday, in the wee hours of the morning, Hattie jammed her one piece of luggage underneath the bottom of the bus, stuffed her ticket in a side zipper of her carry-on bag after she climbed on board, and waved goodbye to her son. After arguing for the last two nights about whether Isaiah was going to "allow" her to go, she had him drop her off at the bus station. Her license expired years ago, and she had forgotten how to drive anyway, so that was never an option. Airplanes were expensive and out of the question, since Hattie would rather die before boarding one. With her Bible in hand and purse almost as heavy as her suitcase by her side, she quickly drifted off to sleep, preparing for the lengthy trip.

When Hattie woke up, they were parked at an Ohio rest stop. She wiped the drool from the corner of her mouth after she looked around to see if anyone was watching, and then got off the bus to stretch her legs and grab something to eat. The piece of pound cake and other little snacks in her bag weren't going to do the trick. On the way inside the building, she glanced at the other people who passed by. *What a freak show!*

There was an older lady with a wart the size of a nipple on her chin who kept looking at people sideways. She had painted on way too much winter-green eyeshadow and bright red lipstick. *She looks like a scary Christmas ornament!* Hattie put her hand up to open the door at the same time as it was being pushed on the other side. The slight gesture surprised her, but she was a little more in shock at the sight before her eyes. A young boy of maybe fourteen had a pink, purple, and blue Mohawk. The boy laughed at her expression, one he probably had gotten many times before. *Oh no. He don't love himself.*

By the time Hattie returned from getting a pre-breakfast snack and stopping in the bathroom to pull up her slouching stockings, the bus was nowhere in sight. She had noticed that people were moving in the opposite direction of her, but she never imagined being left behind.

She hysterically looked from left to right for the bus, realized her fate, and then began kicking the air. "My favorite dress, new shoes, new Suave body wash I was gonna try—just gone!" Then something struck her. She immediately patted her pockets and felt dumb when she remembered that she didn't have any, slung her purse down on top of a trash can, and frantically searched through every nook and cranny. "My ticket!" It was like a weight had been dropped on her. Her temples throbbed as she slowly made her way to the pay phone inside.

Ohio's finest witnessed Hattie's meltdown at the rest stop. The officer offered to take her to the nearest train station, in Elyria, since the next bus station was too far of a commute. She readily accepted. This was her first time in a cop car, and hopefully the last. Hattie strapped herself into her seat and jumped every time she heard the radio screaming at him. *Lord, this ain't good for my nerves.* Happy to move on with her trip, Hattie tried to pay the cop for the ride once they reached their destination, but he refused.

After buying a round-trip ticket for herself and a one-way ticket for her grandson, she sat down on a vacant bench outside. While waiting for the train's arrival, a man with a tight black leather coat and a fedora two sizes too small walked up and plopped down next to Hattie, damn near sitting on her lap. She looked up from her Bible. *If this man's coat gets any tighter, he'll suffocate!* she chuckled to herself.

"Give me your purse," he murmured.

Hattie looked the man up and down before responding. "Get on 'way from me," and continued reading.

"Lady, I'm not asking. I'm telling you." He looked side to side to see if he'd piqued anyone's curiosity.

"Well, I ain't in the mood," she snapped.

"Does this help?" The man stuck a gun in her side; it molded into her squishy flesh.

"Would you like that gift-wrapped?" she questioned, startled by the sudden gesture.

The man angled his back so nobody could see what he was doing. He looked very uncomfortable holding his weapon. *I bet I can take this young punk. He can't even hold it right. Naw, I better keep my cool. I wouldn't look so cool with a bullet in my behind.* Usually people found her size intimidating, but this was the first time her weight hadn't worked to her advantage.

Hattie moaned in defeat and picked the purse up off of the other side of the bench to hand it over. He snatched it from her. *My keys, coupons, Pepto—gone like the Suave!*

"Here! Do you want this too?" She held up her Bible. The man broke off into a sprint, pushing people out of the way and knocking over suitcases. "You need it," she yelled after him, but was easily drowned out by the train's noisy arrival.

One worker inside called security after he heard screaming from the passengers outside, Hattie being the loudest. Tears rolled down her fat cheeks as she explained what went down to security. Naturally, they told her that there wasn't anything that they could do since the man escaped on foot. They did call the police, but Hattie feared they wouldn't show up in time.

"Well, what good are you?" she huffed as she sluggishly hiked up the train's steps, scared she was going to miss another departure.

She sat in her assigned seat with nothing left to her but her tickets in hand, hurt pride, and of course, her Bible. Once situated, she touched the inside of her bra to make sure the money she hid in there for emergencies was still intact. *Yup. My $250's still there.* Out of the corner of her eye, she saw an elderly couple staring at her strangely.

"What are you looking at?" Hattie barked. The couple gasped and turned their heads the other way. She took out a handkerchief from her sweater pocket and blew her nose. Still shaken from the day's events, she clutched her Bible in her arms and sat there rocking while reciting the only passage to get her through her trying times. Psalms 23. *The Lord is my Shepherd, I shall not be in want …*

Hattie arrived at her stop in Virginia, close to 9 a.m. Although she was exhausted from all the morning's festivities, she still had one more means of transportation to take to get to her actual destination, and she had until noon to get there. A cab. *What's going to happen next? Somebody's gonna take my girdle? Well, they can have it, cause it's digging the devil out of my hip!* Since she had some time to kill, she decided she would grab some breakfast close to the center.

She got up and stretched while exiting the train. On the last step, she locked eyes with a middle-aged Caucasian man standing three feet away. His bushy mustache made him look a little suspicious, like he was a porn star in another life. The man opened up his long tan overcoat and exposed all of his nakedness. Nothing but a coat, socks, penny loafers, and a wide toothy grin. He then fled the scene and Hattie lost it.

"Oh, Lord Jesus! Satan in the flesh. Sodom and Gomorrah. Lord have mercy on me. Get me outta this place!" She just couldn't take any more nonsense. One passenger behind Hattie helped her to the nearest bench, tried to calm her down, and called a cab for her. She thanked the lady once she could catch her breath.

"You really don't have to stay with me, you know. I'm all right now," Hattie assured her new friend.

"Oh, I insist. That was an awful thing that man did to you. He needs some serious help."

"He needs Jesus."

"That too." The lady chuckled. "I'm waiting for my husband to come and get me. We live six miles from here, but with him driving *two* miles per hour, he probably won't get here for another half an hour."

Hattie laughed along with the woman as she took a long look at her. She reminded Hattie of her late sister, Lisa Anne, whom her daughter was named after. She had succumbed to breast cancer four days before Ruth Anne was born. Their mother went the same way. Hattie and Lisa Anne had been inseparable, and Hattie's depressive state after her death scared her family. They thought she was going to starve her child to death, not to mention herself. A piece of Hattie died that year too.

Tears clouded Hattie's eyes as the woman gently took hold of her hand. Her new friend noticed she lost her attention and tried to revive Hattie's smile. Together, they created small talk while listening to the joys of baking lemon meringue pie from the Cooking Channel on the overhead TV. As predicted, the woman's husband arrived about a half-hour later and she left as Hattie's cab pulled up to take her to Winston Peter Hall Juvenile Detention Center.

*   *   *

"Stay here. This should only take a second."

"Sure."

Hattie stepped out of the car, looked around at the dull, brown building, and silently thanked God she never had to visit her own son at a place like this. She walked in and was immediately greeted by metal detectors and burly cops. Hattie ventured down the long hallway toward a desk where she had to speak through thick glass. Scared for her safety, she moved the quickest she had in all her life. The man in the information booth passed her a clipboard to sign in and instructed her on how to sign her grandson out. They asked her to wait outside for him.

Caught up in her own thoughts, she saw a fairly muscular, handsome, brown-skinned young man headed in her direction, holding a small box containing his belongings. He smiled a smile that would both melt and break young women's hearts. Despite all the trouble that it took for her to get where she was, she wouldn't trade this joyous occasion of finally meeting her grandson for the world.

"Grandma?"

"My baby!" They embraced, with Hattie almost squeezing the life out of Christopher. She let go of him and held his mannish baby face between her palms. "Oh, you have Ruth Anne's eyes."

"Ruth Anne?"

"Yeah. Your uncle, Isaiah, would be so happy to finally meet you. And I can't wait to get you home to fatten you up!" She poked his stomach like the Pillsbury Doughboy. They walked toward the cab.

Christopher smiled widely, happy to finally leave and looking forward to some home-cooked meals, among other things. He paused and had a puzzled look on his face. "I have an uncle?"

"Yeah, silly. Thought sure your mama would've told you about him. They were as thick as thieves!" she gushed.

"But mama told me that she was the only child."

"'Deed she wasn't! Whatchu talkin' 'bout, boy?" Hattie placed an arm around Christopher. "Well, I guess she felt that way. We haven't seen or talked to her in ages. I'm just so happy to finally meet you!"

Christopher removed his arm from his grandmother's back and reached in his shirt pocket. "I have a picture of her. It's kind of old though. It was taken when I was about two or three. This is the only picture I've got of her. So she's with me every day, whether she wants to be or not." Christopher unfolded it and handed it to Hattie.

She frowned. "Where's this?" She focused on the unfamiliar territory instead of the faces.

He smiled. "Don't you remember? You took it. This was in front of your old house in Cleveland. I don't know how you ended up in Michigan, or should I say, when. Probably the last time I saw you."

"Cleveland?"

"Yeah. She always told me about how you and granddad grew all that corn and okra in your backyard cause 'fresh is always better.'" He chuckled to himself.

Hattie's face scrunched up. "The backyard? Please. Our backyard was as big as a dime! And whose child was this?" Finally zeroing in on the people, she flipped the picture onto the back to search for any writing. "Ruth Anne was tall, skinny, and had long hair. This woman here hadn't combed her hair in weeks! Even though I haven't seen her in years, I know she hasn't changed *this* much. Plus, my child has a birthmark on her right arm that looks like a bruise. Where's that?"

"Birthmark?" Christopher shook his head. "The only thing on her right arm is a tattoo of a fist with the middle finger up."

Hattie nearly swallowed her tongue. They were now within arm's reach of the cab. "Tattoo? A vulgar tattoo? All those years of singing in the choir, Sunday school, Bible study." She paused. "Now wait a minute. Son, what's your mama's name?"

"Juanita." He looked at her like she had just grown two heads from not knowing her own child's name.

All of Hattie's religion went out the window. "Juanita? Cleveland? A tattoo? Who the hell are you? And after all I've been through! I got left at a rest stop, mugged at the train station, flashed by some heathen while getting *off* the train, and now you're telling me that you're not my grandson? Why did you do this to me? Huh? How did you even find me?"

"I looked you up on the internet under 'Atkins.' It said 'Atkins, H. M.,' and my mama always said that my grandmama's name was Harriet Marie," he stuttered, still not completely aware of why she was so upset.

"My name ain't no damn Harriet Marie. Do I *look* like a Harriet? It's Hattie Mae!"

Christopher was stunned and wore a vacant look on his face. "Oh. My bad. Well, can you at least give me a ride still? You shouldn't have to make this trip for nothing."

Hattie flashed him a repulsive smirk as she attacked him with her Bible as a response. Once she got tired of chasing him around the cab, she got in and told the driver to take her back to the train station.

The cab driver, who was sorry to see the show end, pulled off, leaving Christopher in the dust.

Hattie sat back, fuming about the whole situation, but also felt a touch of guilt. She thought about how her "grandson" had nowhere else to go and how happy she had been when she thought her prayers had finally been answered.

Hattie told the driver to stop. He backed up, but not before he rolled his eyes. The car stopped in front of Christopher, who still hadn't moved, and she rolled the window down halfway.

"Get your Black ass in this car," she commanded through clenched teeth. He smiled and hopped in on the other side. *Bastard. Now I'ma have to say a special prayer on behalf of my behavior and language, cause Lord knows that I ain't through kickin' his ass.*

Picnic Ants

Clothe yourselves with compassion, kindness, humility, gentleness, and patience. (Colossians 3:12)

Sister Caroline stood up from the pew, pointed her crooked index finger at Hattie, and spewed, "She should *not* be allowed to enter the cook-off because she's one of the best cooks in the city. We all know that." Her pointy nose, equipped with a booger-looking mole at the tip, reminded Hattie of the Wicked Witch from *The Wizard of Oz* in more ways than one. She was one of the most despised women in the church. Caroline never had anything good to say, unless it was about herself.

Hattie stood in her defense. "How *you* gonna tell me what I can or cannot do, Caroline?" she straightened her shawl before it slipped off her broad shoulders. She continued, "Besides, I already decided not to participate."

The sanctuary filled with panicky mumbling. There were only eight of them on the event committee, but with all the grunts and grovels, you would've thought they were three times that size.

"You can't do that, Sister Hattie," Sister Gertrude interjected, becoming the spokesperson for the mumblers. "I've been looking forward to your sweet potato pie and macrimony and cheese for months!" Sister Gertrude could not say the word "macaroni" to save her life. "My grandbabies are making a special trip up here just for that. What are we supposed to do now?" A few members cheered Gertrude on in agreement.

"*I'm* making the macaroni this year," Sister Caroline chimed in. She placed her bony hand on her hip.

"Now I know what I'm giving up for lent," whispered Lester. Brother Lester was one of the eldest members of the church. He always attempted to whisper, but everybody could still hear every one of his raspy words. Most chuckled. Sister Caroline glared at him.

Pastor Stanley rose to his feet. "Let's all settle down now. Sister Hattie, I would have to agree with Sister Caroline on this one when she said that you are the best cook in the city."

"*One* of," Caroline grumbled and folded her arms in contempt.

He continued. "So, would you consider being one of the judges instead?"

The committee looked at Hattie as if they were watching a tennis match. She hesitated before speaking, then looked up at the ceiling as if it would show her the correct answer. "Well, I guess I could, Pastor."

He smiled a big Kool-Aid smile. Of course he was disappointed like the rest that she wouldn't be preparing the macaroni this year, but he hoped he could get her to do something. "And then perhaps you could make something for the bake sale. You know, we could really use the money to help build a decent kitchen here so that you wouldn't have to cook at home and lug everything in. With your cakes and pies, we should pull in at least a couple hundred on them alone."

"How about a cool million," Brother Lester cracked, imitating a character from Eddie Murphy's classic *Coming to America*.

"So, what do you think?"

"Well, I guess I could whip up some sweet potato pies for your family, Sister Gertrude, and throw in some peach cobbler, lemon pound cake with lemon icing, cherry pie, brownies, and a pineapple upside-down cake." The group sat frozen with their mouths gaped wide open, close to drooling. "That sound okay?"

Pastor Stanley's stomach growled, breaking him out of his trance. "Oh, um, yeah, that'll be wonderful. Moving on to the events."

The meeting went on for another thirty minutes. They discussed everything from who was in charge of the talent show, to who was going to monitor the potato sack race for the kids, to who was going to get dunked first in the dunk tank—the pastor or Trustee Bird. Hattie voted for Bird to go first because she felt he needed to be sanitized in some holy water. He was one of the biggest crooks Hattie had ever met. But she was outnumbered. The majority voted for Pastor to go first in order to save the best for last.

Hattie led the pack and strolled out of the sanctuary with her best friend, Sister Beatrice (aka Sis Bea); Sister Pauline and Sister Gertrude were in tow. Once they hit the pavement, Hattie took her gray and red checkered handkerchief out of her purse and dabbed at the beads of sweat drawn from the sun beaming off her forehead. The ladies cackled and gossiped about the day's events—of course, outside of the church doors. Only heathens sinned in the church.

Hattie called out to Christopher, who was practicing his jump shot on the neighboring basketball court. His muscular six-foot-three frame made him a shoo-in for any pro team, along with his skills of course, as long as they overlooked his criminal record. Even though a year had passed, Hattie still didn't trust a convict to be alone in her house. She dragged Christopher everywhere she went. If you asked her why an eighteen-year-old needed a babysitter, she would change the subject without fessing up to her prejudices.

The ladies parted ways. Christopher opened Hattie's door to let her in and then popped the trunk to toss his basketball in. The thud made Hattie jump. "Christopher!" He looked at her. "You know my nerves are bad."

"Sorry, Grandma."

Hattie plopped down on the Malibu's cloth passenger seat, causing the car to sway like a boat. Christopher closed the door gently behind her and walked around the car to get behind the wheel. As he started pulling out of the parking space, Hattie put in her request. "I need to go to the store. Got a lot of baking to do."

"Why? The picnic's in two weeks, ain't it? 'Sides, it's gonna be a mess since it's Memorial Day weekend."

She looked at him and waited until he was done before cutting into him like a cake. "The day that I get questioned by you or anybody else would be the day that I am six feet deep. Now, take me to the store, and I don't want to hear nothing else unless you ask how fast you should go."

"Yes, ma'am." Christopher did as he was told. He even managed to keep his mouth shut when she asked if he was "crazy" because he ran a yellow light and almost hit a pedestrian. Christopher was in no rush to go shopping, knowing that Hattie's trips took no less than an hour and a half *with* a grocery list. Minus a list—it was over. So, add in the holiday rush, plus her shopping for fifty 'leven church members and their families. He knew he would miss at least an hour or two of his friend's pool party, which was five hours away. But who has a party on a Thursday night anyway?

Christopher steered a full shopping cart behind a lady and her baby in lane thirteen. The cashier was almost finished ringing up her groceries when the lady started fighting tooth and nail for a sale price that expired yesterday. Meanwhile, the woman's child sitting in the buggy smiled at Hattie. She reciprocated. She was then sandwiched between Brother Charles from church and the baby. They caught each other's eyes.

"Oh, uh, Sister Hattie. How are you doing this evening?" His bald Milk Dud-looking scalp shone with sweat. If Hattie didn't know any better, she would've thought that Brother Charles didn't want to be this up close and personal with her.

"Hi'ya doing, Brother Charles. You doing all right?"

"Yeah. I mean, yes, I'm all right," he stuttered. Then the truth was set free.

"What's wrong, baby?" a strawberry-blond curly-haired woman asked. She walked up next to her boo and followed his eyes until they settled on a shocked Hattie. "Oh! Hi, Sister Hattie. What a surprise," she nervously chuckled.

Hattie had heard rumors about Brother Charles dating a younger woman, but it was now confirmed that the forty-year-old was indeed smooching up on the twenty-something Sister Lea, aka Miss Lay. Word was, she got more play than the church's organ. Hattie spoke, turned her attention to her groceries spread across the store's conveyor belt, and added a mental note in her head to call Sis Bea as soon as she got home.

Once Hattie and Christopher hit the front door, the phone rang. Christopher sprinted to answer it, dropping two full grocery bags on the floor, tripping Hattie. Luckily for her, she grabbed onto the foyer's entrance table to keep from falling; luckily for him, Hattie wouldn't have to beat him for sending her plummeting to the floor. *He will get fussed at regardless, that's for sure.*

"Grandma, it's for you," Christopher yelled out while covering the receiver with his sticky palm; he had been tearing up some sour candy in the car. Even though the Malibu was his, Hattie told him not to be eating in her car. Christopher did what he was told and placed the bag in the cup holder.

Hattie waddled to the phone, fussing—*didn't even get in the house good and gettin' bags thrown at me. Know what, them eggs better not be broke!* The creaky wooden floor played like a soundtrack with each heavy step she took. Once Christopher handed her the phone, he leaped over the phone cord and made sure that every item from every bag was put away nice and neat. He figured that if he did everything else right, he wouldn't get it as bad.

"Hello," Hattie flopped down in her favorite chair. The cushion hissed. She picked up her pen to take notes, just in case.

"Mama."

"Isaiah, is that you?"

"Yeah, Mama. Who else? I got your messages."

"I hate talking to that ole answering thang of yours. Where have you been? I was about to put your face on the side of a milk carton."

Isaiah sighed. He knew his mother wasn't playing. "I was out of town."

"Where? And with who? You need to tell me these things, cause if something would've happened—"

He cut in. "But nothing did. I'm fine and had a great time in Miami."

"Whatchu go down there for? You can't see alligators up here? You know we got a zoo now."

Isaiah shook his head as if she could see his frustration. "I didn't see no alligators. I went to meet up with a friend."

"What kind of friend? A woman?"

"Yeah, Ma. A woman." Hattie huffed in disapproval. She still treated him as if he were ten years old instead of forty. "Her name is Raine and—"

"Raine? What kind of name is that for a grown woman?" She briefly paused. "She Black? Better be well over 21."

Unable to hold back any longer, "Yes, Ma! Dang, you are some kind of killjoy, you know that? That's why I didn't tell you before I left."

"Well, excuse me for caring about my child. She must be some kind of special to get you to travel eight hundred miles. I can't even get you to go to the store for me half the time."

"I was not that far, Mama. And I guess she is 'kind of special.' We have a lot in common and I enjoy her company."

"Why don't she come up here to visit? You know I gotta check her out."

"Uh, maybe later. I'm coming over next Sunday for dinner."

"Like you had a choice." Isaiah grunted at his mother's smart remark. "Pastor Stanley elected me to be a judge for the picnic instead of cooking for it. You know it's in two weeks."

"You're not cooking?" he asked frantically.

She beamed. "Yes; well, in a way. I'll be doing the bake sale; baking and running it. You gon' have to bring your calculator. You know I can't subtract good."

"Yes, Mama."

"And bring your lil friend too."

Isaiah rolled his eyes, grateful they were on the phone, because if she ever caught him doing it in person, his eyes would have rolled by themselves back down to Miami. "I'll try, Mama."

"Good. Well, I gotta go warm up these leftovers. Sister Caroline conveniently forgot to bring some snacks to the meeting today, with her cheap self. She could've picked up a bag of chips or something."

"You know it *is* a recession."

"Recess my foot!" He didn't bother to correct her. "We all had our stomachs grumbling, mumbling, and fumbling. Shoot. Well, let me get the gettin'. I'll see you later. Glad you're above ground, son."

He snickered. "Me too, Mama."

They said their "I love yous" and "good nights" before they hung up. It took Hattie longer to heat up the wild rice, greens, fried chicken, mashed potatoes, and cornbread than it took her and her grandson to clean their plates.

* * *

The following week came and went in the blink of an eye. And before they knew it, it was the night before the main event. Hattie wasn't a bit worried, but Sis Bea couldn't say the same. Hattie lost track of how many pep talks she had to give her to encourage her to stay in the cook-off. Sis Bea counted on her vote, and Hattie secretly prayed that Bea's dish would be good enough so she wouldn't have to pick someone else over her best friend whom she loved like a sister. Not that she wasn't a good cook, but Hattie knew from experience that Bea's cooking could taste a little like fresh brick from time to time.

Hattie had completely worn herself out with all the cooking and baking she did for her family and for the picnic. Anybody who walked in her kitchen now would think that a tornado touched down. The rest of her house was immaculate, but she couldn't help dirtying almost every dish she owned. From the brownies to the cherry, apple, and sweet potato pies; from the chocolate chip cookies to the pound and pineapple upside-down cakes, her blood sugar increased by merely looking at the buffet. Hattie put the final touches on her desserts and took a good hard look at the mess she'd made. There were sugar and flour patches on the tan ceramic floor, a sink full of spoons and bowls, egg shells scattered on the kitchen island along with droplets of milk and dabs of butter. Her clothes and apron wore the same ingredients.

Luckily, Isaiah had remodeled Hattie's kitchen for her sixty-fifth birthday two years ago, and the floor was much easier to clean. So she did what any other exhausted woman would do: she called in her grandson to make her place spick-and-span again. He mumbled about being awakened out of some great sleep, but not loud enough for Hattie to hear, and then she went to bed.

* * *

Finally, the day had come. The children couldn't wait to play with their church friends; young men and ladies could pretend like they were talking about Jesus instead of other less Godly stuff; the older women folk could show off their church hats; and the men could fill their bellies like it was Thanksgiving. Hattie looked forward to making a profit off of the three days she spent prepping and baking. She didn't want the money personally; she simply wanted to contribute to the place she called home. No, it wasn't where she laid her head at night, but Faithful God, Our Heavenly Savior & Glory Methodist

Church was where she spent the majority of her time worshiping, praying, singing, and loving thy neighbor—except for a couple of heffas. Hattie loved to sing and tried to strong-arm her way into the choir until she was strongly advised to stick to cooking, but she didn't care. She shrugged it off as jealousy and still sang the loudest and the foulest in the sanctuary.

Packing up the car on the way to the picnic was a fiasco! Hattie fussed every time the front or car door opened or closed. *"Be careful holding that. You're gonna let all the flies in. You're not carrying that right. Don't you drop that!"* You would think that neither Isaiah nor Christopher could breathe right. Then the inevitable happened. Isaiah took the last cooler out to his SUV and Christopher had a stack of the last six pies that couldn't fit into the coolers in his hands. A bee buzzed around his pockets; must've smelled either his cologne or some candy. Christopher got nervous and did a weird dance to move away from the bee. The annoying little insect circled him and went back to his pocket. Instead of ignoring the pest, Christopher jerked away; his body went one way, and the pie on top went another. Isaiah and Hattie froze.

To make matters worse, Hattie tripped over her own foot and stepped right into the fallen sweet potato pie that otherwise would've been alright to eat since it was still wrapped. The now demolished pie added fuel to the fire. Hattie chased Christopher around the car, swinging her Bible. Once she tired herself out, Isaiah brought her a change of stockings and shoes. Everybody got into the car and went on about their business. Hattie wasn't a bit embarrassed that some of her neighbors watched her shenanigans. *They should be used to me by now.*

The Atkins family was the last of the committee members to arrive at the picnic, as usual. Hattie was told to be there at ten, but she strolled in at ten forty-five. It was a beautiful day for a gathering. The sun wasn't too hot just yet; some clouds were out, paired with a soft breeze every few minutes. The open field behind the church was full of booths that were soon to be packed with families. Hattie was given a card table to set her desserts on until she almost made Trustee Bird's wife cry. "What am I 'posed to do with that? Deborah, are you serious?" She was then awarded with two picnic tables and could not stop smiling. Anybody who didn't know that Hattie was a perfectionist, especially when it came to her cooking, would think that she was just a mean old bat.

She opened up an old pale blue bedsheet and draped it over the tables. Figuring she wouldn't have any extra room for decorations and such, she hadn't packed any. Hattie set up quite a beautiful spread for her customers. When she was finally done setting up, she sat down on her lawn chair, pulled her floppy straw hat down over her eyes, and took a nap. She was pooped.

Half an hour later, Christopher woke her up. Some of the church members had arrived and were ready for dessert. She jolted, folding her chair up around herself.

"Help! Somebody help me! Lord Jesus!" Christopher and Brother Phillip grabbed her arms and pulled her out of the half-folded seat.

"You all right, Sister Hattie?" Brother Phillip asked worriedly.

"I'm alright. I thought the good Lord done snatched me up!"

Christopher shook his head. "You sure you alright, Grandma?" He propped open the chair again for her.

"Get that death trap away from me. I ain't sitting back in that thing so it can swallow me whole!" Christopher folded it up and leaned it against a tree.

People were still laughing, but they were also further away so Hattie couldn't see specific faces. She scolded Christopher for scaring three years of life out of her and for not waking her earlier. She then "punished" him by making him handle the money from the sales. "No stealing, you hear me," were the last words she said to him before putting on her happy face for her customers/friends.

They worked as a team, Hattie dishing out her delicious treats and Christopher collecting the money. But this got old to Christopher after an hour. He wanted to join his friends and kick it with his new girlfriend. Hattie told him to have his friends come over to eat or else he wouldn't be "kicking" nothing. So, he did as he was told. He texted his friends to come over to the dessert table as soon as Hattie left for the restroom.

On her way back from the ladies' room, a couple of people stopped Hattie to speak, catch up, and rave about her baked goods. Everyone was having a fabulous time, including Pastor Stanley, who was in the dunk tank. So far, he had only been dunked twice and still wore a smile on his handsome face. However, she stopped dead in her tracks when she heard a young girl say she got a free slice of pie. Hattie looked in the girl's direction 'cause she just knew that she wasn't talking about *her* pie. Sure enough, the hussy was chowing down on her Granny Smith apple pie. Hattie started to confront the girl, but then she decided against it and instead headed right to the source.

"Christopher!" The gang of teenagers surrounding the dessert table scattered like roaches. They knew what time it was.

It was written all over Christopher's face that he'd given that pie away, and maybe others. Drenched in guilt, he attempted to smile and greet her, but bet against it. "Yes, Grandma?"

"What the hell are you doing giving away free pie?" Hattie could hear "oohhs" behind her, but she didn't care that she was loud or that she'd just cussed on church property. She simply didn't give a damn.

"Everyone paid, Grandma." He swallowed hard and felt like a minnow inches away from a shark.

Hattie stepped closer and got in his face and pointed in the opposite direction. "Then that polka dot heffa is eatin' someone else's apple pie?" By then they had drawn a small crowd, but the spectators didn't get *too* close. Everyone knew to keep their distance when Hattie went on her tangents.

Some instigator tapped the apple gobbler on the shoulder, since she appeared in the crowd. "Well, how much is it?" she asked.

Hattie's head whipped around. She never liked nosy people, especially people who interrupted her. "Check your tone, young lady, check your tone. I wouldn't even worry about it. But don't ignore the concept of a bake *sale*, okay. When someone is selling something, that usually means that it's not free." She turned back to Christopher. "Besides, all your little 'hook-ups' will be coming out of *your* pocket. I expect my money by the end of the day. *And* more importantly, you're fired. Back up away from my tables!"

There weren't many who weren't laughing. Christopher hung his head and disappeared into the crowd. The apple gobbler sucked her teeth at Hattie to try to save face, but everybody knew the deal. After that showdown, Hattie collected quite a bit in tips.

The children were having a ball over at the racing section toward the back of the park. If they weren't racing in the potato sacks, then they were racing with water balloons. Each relay was sectioned off by cones, signs, and people. Pastor had never seen a crowd so huge with such excitement in his Sunday services.

The dunk tank was doing almost as well as the dessert table. Since Pastor Stanley switched with Trustee Bird, the line had extended to the parking lot! There were plenty of people who looked like pros when they threw those balls close to his head. Needless to say, Bird could barely get seated before he was dropped back into the water. He almost cussed out the Wallace family as Sister Janet, her husband, three children, and two nephews dunked Bird back-to-back.

"Sister Hattie!" She looked over to see who was calling and found Pastor Stanley heading in her direction with his teenage son, Michael. "Sister, are you ready to judge some good eats?"

She smiled, secretly wishing that the Clifton Davis lookalike was single. Pastor Stanley's daddy, whose church he took over, was just as fine. She spoke to Michael before responding to him. "Do grasshoppers hop?"

Pastor instructed Michael to manage the dessert tables and walked with Hattie over to the judge's table. Trustee Ubert was already seated.

Surprise, surprise. Ubert wasn't nicknamed "Universe" for nothing, but of course that was behind his back. They made sure to give him bite-sized portions or else there would be nothing left for anyone else to taste. Hattie and Ubert spoke, and then she took her seat between Pastor and Ubert. Pastor Stanley read the rules for the competition aloud before they were advised to "dig in." There were three bowls put in front of them; the table was dressed for royalty. Gold tablecloth, napkins, silverware, bibs, confetti, and seat cushions. Brother Abe, Sis Bea's husband, fanned the judges with a giant pink feather. *Am I on my way out or what?*

The "Wicked Witch" had made some macaroni and cheese as promised, and it was awful. It had too much milk and too little cheese. Hattie grimmed her. *She probably did that on purpose. Damn, she's a terrible cook. Next!*

Next was Sis Bea's spaghetti and meatballs. She looked deeply upset, and Hattie could understand why—she forgot the damn meatballs! Otherwise, it was mediocre at best. It could stand some more spices, *any* spices, but it was still better than Caroline's.

And lastly, one of the newest church members made an enormous pot of greens. Hattie looked at Serenity and almost laughed right in her baby face. She was sitting there just grinning with her husband, Patrick. *What do these youngins know about greens? And why are they smiling like that? I ain't no dentist! This better be good.*

Trustee Ubert tasted a forkful of greens first. Both Hattie and Pastor looked at him to gauge his expression.

"Ummm, this is really good," he pointed his fork to the empty bowl that formerly housed his greens.

"I haven't seen food you haven't liked, Ubert," Hattie cracked. Everyone laughed, except ole sourpuss Caroline, of course.

"No, for real. Try it and you'll see. Try it!"

Pastor tasted his next. "Wow. Brother Ubert, you're right!" He buried the unchewed in his cheek, looked at Sister Serenity, and joked, "Young lady, you put your *foot* in these greens!" The couple laughed. Hattie tasted hers and sided with the men, agreeing that Sister Serenity won hands down.

"What? She won!" Caroline hollered. "I can't believe this! Can't no little girl cook no greens that good!"

"Well, she did *and* she won," Hattie sniped. "Matter of fact, she could probably show you a thing or two."

"Give it here." Caroline grabbed a fork and sampled the greens herself, right out of the pot. She tried to hide her pleasure by smirking. "It's aiight."

"Well, I could add some—" Serenity started.

Hattie cut in. "Don't even bother listening to that ole hen. It's fine the way it is." Hattie turned her nose up at Ubert when he gulped down the greens' juice from his bowl.

"Yeah, quit hatin'." Pastor grabbed a spoon and put two large spoonfuls in his bowl. "We're gonna have to have you cook for more functions, Sister Serenity." Hattie looked up. "Alongside Sister Hattie, of course. We'll draw in even more members. Also, don't forget to join our Young Adult ministry. We'd love to have you." Pastor provided more details of the ministry to the young couple as they enjoyed him taking a few minutes to speak with them on a personal level. Pastor Stanley was a huge part of why folks stayed at this church; his charming personality, thoughtfulness, good looks, and commanding voice were the icing.

Silently fuming, Sis Bea took the spoon out of her spaghetti and tried to knock the remainder off on the side of the dish. A noodle inadvertently jumped out of the bowl and landed on Sister Caroline's hand.

"So what, you're throwing stuff now?" Sister Caroline asked nastily. "Grow up, Bea. You lost too." She flicked what was stuck to her dry macaroni spoon at Sis Bea. Bea's bug eyes grew to the size of saucers before she threw the closest thing to her, a cup, at Caroline. Instead of returning fire to Bea—or doing nothing at all—Caroline flicked some of her tasteless noodles at a laughing Serenity. Everyone was in shock.

Hattie got up from the table before any food got on her—that would have been game over.

"Ah, hell naw!" *Uh oh. This child's about to get buck!* Hattie stole a quick glance back at the unfolding scene while grabbing a chicken leg or two at the next table.

"Wait, babe. Let's think about this." Patrick attempted to calm the situation, but instead got put right in the middle of it when some crispy mac and cheese noodles smacked his cheek. "Nev'mind, let's get 'em!"

Within seconds, a couple of handfuls of the spaghetti was worn on Patrick, Serenity, Bea, and Caroline's clothes. Red splotches were also in their hair and on their faces, making them look like they just stepped out of a slasher movie. The macaroni didn't do any damage, except for when it whipped against each other's faces and got under their fingernails. And everyone just got wet with the greens.

Serenity threw a handful of greens at Caroline, which hit her right by her pelvic bone and slid down, making her look like she'd peed on herself. Hattie cracked up as she sat eating at a safe distance. Ubert never budged. Obviously, he didn't care about getting hit with anything. He was more concerned about not breaking away from the food he'd scooped before the fight.

"Enough!" Pastor Stanley hollered, breaking up the food fight that was inching closer to an all-out brawl. Once the small crowd around them dispersed, the fighters solemnly walked into the church to get cleaned up. Pastor followed and grabbed Brother Ubert for backup in case anything else popped off.

Hattie finished her plate, glanced over her shoulder at her dessert tables, and saw that Michael was doing okay, so she walked over to the dozen rows of chairs that were set up for the talent show. As soon as she found a seat and got comfortable, Christopher went over to her, hugged her as a peace offering, and sat next to her. She smiled and draped her arm around him, thinking that everything was going to be alright. Nope!

Once every seat was filled, the judges took their seats up front. Hattie knew off rip that the event was doomed when she saw who had been chosen to be the judges: Brother Charles, Brother Malcolm, and Sister Beverly. To anyone else, those elected may have *looked* impartial, but Hattie knew what was up. Sister Lay's sister was in the show, so it wouldn't take a rocket scientist to know who Brother Charles was voting for. Hattie overheard Brother Malcolm speaking to Brother Phillip right before the cook-off and saw Phillip slip Malcolm a twenty. Brother Phillip's bow-legged stepson was also in the show. Malcolm was probably paid not to laugh or to judge him too harshly for not having any rhythm.

Sister Beverly was a different story. She was the only one who had no ties to the contestants and didn't accept any bribes from anyone. She was also the only panelist who was blind in one eye and cockeyed in the other. Why would they put that kind of pressure on someone who can't see worth a damn? Did they not realize that she could be judging an audience member for all they knew?

Everyone quieted down once Isaiah took the stage as the emcee. Of all the talent show committee members, he had the best stage presence. He looked especially handsome in his cream linen suit. He grabbed the microphone and turned on his gentlemanly charm.

"Good afternoon, brothers and sisters, and little ones. How is everyone doing on this hot June afternoon?" In response, Isaiah got some applause, "alrights," and even a couple of winks. Isaiah took out his brown handkerchief and dabbed his forehead before continuing. "Welcome to Faithful God, Our Heavenly Savior & Glory Methodist Church's third annual picnic and talent show. This is the part I *know* everybody's been waiting for, cause this show is far better than *American Idol.*" Isaiah laughed at his weak attempt at a joke, but was somewhat serious. He knew that some extraordinary talent began in a church and hoped that one day, theirs would be put on the map. He continued, "We have a fine lineup for you today. So we'll get the show started with the Joann sisters—JoJo, Alicia, and Nini! Give it up, y'all."

The audience cheered as the girls took the stage. The crowd wasn't as hyped once they finished, for all the humping, jiggling, and gyrating that was going on. They earned their five out of ten stars. Sad thing was, their score was only that high out of sympathy.

Next was the Jazzy Squad: a few young couples who decided to showcase their ballroom dancing skills. This was nice and refreshing to see, especially after what had just been witnessed and what was sure to come. The only gripe Hattie had was that some of the girls' dresses were a tad too short for a church function. At one point, one girl did a turn and someone commented a little too loudly, "She don't have no drawers on!" The girl, obviously embarrassed, quickly smoothed her dress down, but the damage had been done. She kept a hand at the hem of her dress for the duration of the song.

The next two acts were similar to the first, but not quite as graphic, including Sister Lay's sister. There was a soloist and an all-girl singing group that were both bland at best. Brother Phillip's stepson, Evan, danced last. It took him a while to hit the stage after he was introduced, which led most of the spectators to believe that he had been forced to participate. The boy reluctantly appeared on stage and provided the comedy everyone was anticipating.

Evan began by tripping over the microphone cord and landing in almost the middle of the stage. He straightened out his crooked glasses, introduced himself, and backed up to center stage. "You Be Illin'" by Run-D.M.C. cued up and scared the lame boy half to death. He jumped and started breakdancing, if that's what you could call it. His lanky arms and legs appeared identical to Sis Bea's spaghetti noodles, and he looked like a five-year-old dancing instead of the twelve he was. Everybody, including Sister Caroline, busted out laughing. But not Hattie. She watched Evan in horror and amazement. In the middle of the song, Evan got up off of the floor and exited the stage. People weren't sure if they should clap or not, *or if he left because they* were laughing or because he ran out of moves. Isaiah answered the first question by appearing on stage and asking for the audience to "Give it up one more time."

After a few minutes of deliberation, the judges were ready to announce their decision. Sister Beverly was the spokesperson and stood to her feet. Isaiah handed her the microphone.

"Although there was a lot of tough competition this year, we the judges decided that Evan Mathews is our third-place winner, the Jazzy Squad came in a close second, and Michelle Jeffries won first prize!" Half of the crowd clapped. Sister Lay sashayed through the crowd and walked onto the stage to congratulate her sister on stealing the show.

"Are you kidding?" A voice from the back shouted. Once Brother Ubert moved, Hattie could see that it was one of the choir members, Sister Anita. "You crooked-eyed bitty can't even see that that heffa ain't got no talent. Y'all better look again!"

Sister Lay couldn't fake or hide her embarrassment. She grabbed her stunned little sister and led her off the stage. Sister Beverly immediately sat down in her seat with tears threatening to fall. The spectators standing around Sister Anita laughed at her insults, which egged her on.

"That dance group had the most talent. They practiced and er'thang. And that lil ole boy looked like he was getting electrocuted or sumthin'."

Pastor Stanley tried to calm the crowd, but the name-calling, yelling, and laughter drowned his voice. Hattie got up, told Christopher to "come on," and squeezed herself through the aisle. She headed straight to the front. Christopher tried to stop her for fear of even more embarrassment, but he was swatted away. Hattie slowly climbed the stage steps and took the mic from the stand before Isaiah could.

"Testing, testing." Hattie tapped on the microphone to make sure it was still on before she shouted out, "Hey!" The crowd stopped dead in their tracks and looked up at her. "What's the matter with y'all? Y'all forgettin' that these are just kids up here? It's only a stupid lil contest. Who cares if Sister Beverly is as blind as a bat or Evan can't dance. Who cares! Let these chil'ren be! The judges made their decision and that's that. I don't wanna hear no mo arguing; makes me nervous. Y'all know I got bad nerves. Now, the picnic's over—ain't it, Pastor?"

Pastor Stanley spoke up from the crowd. "Yes, yes it is, Sister Hattie."

"So y'all go around here and pick up all this shit—I mean, shoot, stuff up. Y'all know what I'm tryna say! Clean up, go home, and go to bed." Hattie tried to put the microphone back on the stand, but it wasn't working out. Frustrated, she threw it on the stage. The crowd hollered at the loud shrieking noises. On its way down, the mic picked up some more choice words of Hattie's that weren't meant for a church setting. Isaiah snatched up the screeching microphone and placed it back on the stand, helped his mother down the stairs, and went with her to clean up and shut down her dessert area.

Who knew that a food fight, corrupt judges, and fighting families would all be a part of a church picnic? *Welp, can't wait till next year!*

Is This the End?

"For this reason a man will leave his father and mother and be united to his wife, and the two will become one flesh." So they are no longer two, but one. Therefore what God has joined together let man not separate.
(MATTHEW 19:5-6)

"Chris. Christopher?" Hattie called from upstairs.
"Yeah?"
"'Yeah'? Who you think you talking to, boy?"
"Oops; sorry, ma'am. Yes?"
"That's better. See who's ringing the doorbell this time of morning."
"Okay." Christopher hopped out of bed in hopes he would catch whoever rang the bell three times in a row before they took off. *Whoever it is, I hope they mean business. I'm not gonna take the rap for the paperboy disturbing Grandma. One more thing for her to fuss at.*

He opened the door in time to see a lady in a form-fitting tan sheath from the back. Once she turned, she reminded him of Lena James from *A Different World*. He definitely liked what he saw, and smiled a shy smile. "What can I do for you?" Christopher stepped onto the porch, attempting to close the distance between him and her. The woman only looked at him. Christopher couldn't tell if she was smiling at him or grimacing from the sun shining in her eyes.

"I have a package for Ms. Atkins. Is she home?" She flashed a badge at him—no smile.

"She's inside. I can take you in."

"Um, no thanks."

"Oh, then I can take this for her." Christopher stretched his arms out to take the package. Looking down at her hands allowed him a chance to steal a quick peek at the upper half of her body. He liked.

She cocked an attitude once she noticed Christopher's eyes roaming. "Look, she needs to sign for this. Can you get her, please? Now." The process server sighed heavily, dropped her signature pad noisily by her side, and looked away.

Her attitude shift drenched Christopher like a bucket of cold water. "All right." He stepped back into the house to get Hattie.

"Grandma?" No answer. "GRANDMA," he called out a little louder. He moved to the middle of the kitchen, unsure of where she might be and why she couldn't hear him. Next, he heard the toilet flush. Christopher knew then that it was going to take Hattie another five or ten minutes to shuffle back out, but he decided to call out her name again to push her along.

"What, boy?"

"There's somebody here to see you."

"Who is it?"

"Some lady with a package that she's gotta give to you and you only." Christopher heard splashing water before the bathroom door swung open.

"Package?"

"Yeah." Hattie shot him a look. Even though she was a few feet away from Christopher, he didn't need twenty-twenty vision to see that she hated the word *yeah*. "Yes ma'am."

"Well, where is she?" Hattie hobbled past Christopher and headed to the door. On the way, she straightened her wig, which made her look even worse. She opened the screen door. "How can I help you?"

"Hi ma'am. Just dropping this off for you. Can you sign here, please?"

"Sign? Sign for what?"

"Your package."

"I don't even know what it is. I didn't order anything. Christopher," Hattie glanced over her shoulder. She couldn't see him, but she knew he was there. "You order something?"

"No ma'am."

"I don't know what it is either, ma'am. Could you please sign to say that you received it?" She stuck a clipboard out with a pen attached.

Hattie looked the girl over for a minute and sucked her teeth in disgust. She finally consented, signed the paperwork, and was handed a thick manila envelope. Hattie flipped the package over to look at it on all sides and sniffed it before closing the door.

She waddled into the next room to her favorite spot: her beige corduroy recliner that was worn in the middle and had a white doily on the headrest. Hattie flopped down and carefully opened the package. She pulled out a small stack of papers before reaching over to the end table's drawer and grabbing her reading glasses.

"So what did you get?" Christopher eyed the papers, suddenly getting curious. He hoped that it wasn't his birth mother coming to take him back. Hattie didn't have legal custody of him, so for the last two years or so, he had been waiting for a call, a letter, or something stating that he wasn't where he should be. Even though he was twenty years old, legally an adult now, he always had that thought in the back of his mind. *Can they still take me, as old as I am*? he wondered. But really, if it wasn't for Hattie, he more than likely would've gone to prison by now. As for his mother, he hadn't heard from her since he entered juvie a few years ago.

"Mind your business, boy." Even though Hattie was rough on Christopher, she still loved him as her own. Matter of fact, that was how she showed her love: by fussing. Her son, Isaiah, could attest to that. "Turn that light on for me, please." Christopher did as he was told and sat on the couch across from Hattie. She skimmed over the first sheet and nearly fell out of her seat. "What!"

"What's wrong?"

Hattie didn't answer until she reread the page and went on to the next. And there it was in black and white. "A divorce? This bastard wants a divorce?" Hattie's heart sank, blocking out Christopher's presence.

Hattie hadn't seen Benjamin in over thirty years. He'd been all bundled up with another woman, with his hand on her pregnant belly like a proud papa. They looked happy, just like how Benjamin used to dote on Hattie. On some level, she always believed that he was going to come home, but he never did. Even though the other woman was right there in her face, Hattie still loved him, and she couldn't help but think about how her life would be different if Benjamin was still in it. Maybe she'd still be in Mississippi. Maybe she would've had a bigger family. Maybe her daughter, Ruth Anne, wouldn't have gotten knocked up and kicked out. Tears formed and splattered on the word "dissolution."

She wondered what had changed. "A hundred years later and now he wants a divorce?" *Why am I so surprised? He moved on years ago.* Hattie was raised as a good Christian woman who didn't believe in divorce. What would God think of her blemish? Only a fool would remain faithful to an absent husband after all this time. But she was Benjamin's fool. She couldn't explain it to her children or herself. Love was a bitch.

Hattie put the papers on the coffee table next to her and ignored the envelope that slid off her lap and onto the floor. She stepped on it and shuffled upstairs to her bedroom. Once she was inside her comfortable quarters, she plopped down on the side of her bed and let the tears flow. Granted, Benjamin didn't deserve her tears, but him entering her life again had made her a bit emotional. Benjamin was her children's father, but this was a different kind of pain that Hattie had never experienced. The bittersweet finale.

She sat quietly sobbing for a few minutes, then crossed the room to her closet. On a shelf above her clothes rested some shoeboxes that contained everything but shoes—money, secret recipes, old letters, and receipts. Underneath lay a photo album. She pulled it out and returned to the bed. Hattie opened the album and immediately smiled.

The album held pictures of her and Benjamin from beginning to end. The first picture showed the happy couple sharing a banana split at an ice cream parlor. It was obvious that Benjamin's best friend had had a little too much to drink before taking their photo; the camera was aimed too high and it almost cut Benjamin out of the picture. But it did catch Hattie laughing. She was tickled that Benjamin not only insisted that they take a picture together but also managed to get ice cream on the tip of his nose.

The next picture was them at the roller-skating rink. That was one of her favorites. Hattie smiled and gently stroked the picture, mentally recapturing that day.

*   *   *

"I'm surprised you were able to come out tonight."

"Me too," Hattie beamed. "I was making my mama sick begging to get out of the house." She enjoyed all the attention Benjamin was giving her. He'd dumped his old girlfriend to spend some time with her. Benjamin called her before she got ready for bed, at a respectable time of course. He also walked her home from school, even though he lived in the total opposite direction.

"I got your rental."

"Thank you." She cuffed her arm into his and they walked over to the counter to rent her roller-skates. Benjamin waited patiently. He grabbed Hattie's hand once she was laced up and led her out to the floor. Benjamin talked a good game about being the best skater in town, and Hattie couldn't wait to see firsthand.

The grinning couple skated slowly, hand in hand, sneaking peeks at each other on the straightaways. Benjamin suddenly let go of her hand and slid in front of her. Not only was he showboating his backward skating skills, but he also tried to jazz it up a little bit. He was too busy looking at Hattie to notice the huge six-foot-two grizzly-bear-looking man behind him. Before Hattie could warn him, Benjamin skated back-first into the man. As big as he was, Benjamin only bounced off of him, which led him to fly into her. The couple both landed on the floor with Benjamin on top. They cracked up, as well as everyone else, except for the grizzly. They didn't care that they were laughing for an entirely different reason than everybody else.

Even though Hattie had bumped her head pretty hard, the teenage couple remained in their own puppy love world. Benjamin stopped laughing long enough to deliver his first kiss. The crowd went from giggles to cheers, until an employee broke them up—he thought it might be the beginning of something else. So this particular rink was special; not only did they share their first kiss there, but Benjamin also asked to court her that night. Hattie happily accepted. The first official picture with her new man was of her wrapped in his arms wearing a ring pop to show their commitment.

* * *

"You all right up there?" Christopher called to Hattie. He hadn't heard any movement for a while and was getting worried. He wasn't used to her storming off with tears in her eyes. Fury, yes; plus tears, not so much.

"I'm all right, Christopher. Can you do me a favor?" She didn't wait for an answer. "Can you put a pot on for me?"

"Yes ma'am." Christopher left the bottom of the stairs and headed to the kitchen. The next thing Hattie heard was the banging of pans.

Hattie rose from her seat, wiped her face to make sure she didn't leave any tear residue, and put the album back. She took a couple of slow steps to get herself together before she returned downstairs. Once she reached the living room, she glanced at the clock. *It's five-thirty already? What have I been doing for the last couple of hours?* She didn't realize that she had spent so long reflecting on her past—a past that had now been shoved down her throat.

Hattie heard bubbles coming from the stove. She turned the dial down and grabbed another pan.

"Whatchu gonna make?"

"Spaghetti." Hattie glided around the kitchen and grabbed all the ingredients to prepare for the "best spaghetti in the East" (so she was told by her church family) until she was stopped in her tracks.

"So, why are you so shocked that your old man is divorcing you? You haven't seen or talked to him in years, right?"

Hattie whipped her head around to Christopher. "Why am I shocked? Are you crazy? He is still my husband and—I know I haven't talked to him or—wait, how do you know that I haven't talked to him in years? You been spying on me?" She pointed her wooden spoon at Christopher. He shook his head as she continued. "Look, you just don't understand."

"What don't I understand?"

"Nothing and never mind. Just hush. Gonna tell me," Hattie's voice trailed off.

The kitchen sat quiet for a few, but Christopher had one more question he was itching to get out. "Were you mean to him or something? You ran him off, didn't you?" Christopher knew he was well over the edge, but he had to know what "you just don't understand" was code for. He couldn't be too young to understand. Hell, he was an adult now. So what else could it have been other than her attitude?

Hattie glared at Christopher so hard that he felt like he was five years old in the principal's office. Then, without warning, she snapped.

"Ahh!" Hattie grabbed the pot full of boiling water and hurled it across the room at the wall. Water doused the floor and everything in its path. And just like that, Hattie left the kitchen for her bedroom and did not return.

*   *   *

The house filled with the pleasant scent of brownies that somehow overpowered the pound cake, cheesecake, and yellow sheet cake. Hattie was in a baking mood—which happened every other day, but today, she was going overboard. It was her go-to "what the hell is going on" thinking strategy. Hattie narrowed her focus on baking and ignored all the other sounds around her, such as the phone ringing and Christopher sporadically calling her from his room.

Sweat from her brow plopped onto the counter. Her large frame and the eighty-degree weather without air conditioning was a dangerous combination. Tears joined in with the sweat. She just couldn't wrap her mind around being a divorcee. She hadn't talked to anybody, but she figured she owed it to Isaiah, even though he hadn't seen or spoken to his father in over thirty years either. Hattie wiped her hands on a dish towel, folded it over the oven door handle, then shuffled out of the kitchen.

Christopher stuck his head out of his bedroom door. "Grandma, can I talk to you for a minute?"

Without even looking at him, she replied, "Not right now, baby. I gotta make a call."

Christopher hung his head, then closed the door behind him. Hattie's mind was elsewhere, but he hadn't expected her to totally shut down and cut him off. She'd barely said two sentences to him since she got served three days ago. Last night, they ate in silence in the family room with the television on low volume. She sat in her favorite chair and Christopher sat on her stiff white and pink couch. The room reminded him of a funeral parlor, except the floral arrangements were on the upholstery. The cream-colored drapes and dull brown walls that matched the creaky floorboards made it feel like a coffin. He hated the suffocating house, but loved having a place to call home.

Once Hattie made it to the phone next to her throne, she pressed the number two on her speed dial and, while waiting, she flopped down in her favorite spot. Finally, they connected.

Isaiah sucked his teeth when Hattie muttered a hello. "I've known you for forty-two years now. You can basically call me an expert when it comes to telling what kind of mood you're in. Now, tell me what's wrong. What happened?"

Hattie inhaled and let out an even bigger exhale. "Yeah, you right son. You always right."

"Oh my God. Who's dead!"

"Don't use the Lord's name in vain, boy. I taught you better than that."

Isaiah smiled. "Now that's the Hattie Mae Atkins I know and love. Not whoever just admitted that someone else was right besides herself. Now talk to me, Mama. For real." He teased his mother, but he really was concerned about her. It had been years since she sounded so down and depressed. He wanted her to hurry up and spill the beans, but he also knew that saying the wrong things would automatically shut her down for good.

"I heard from your father."

"You mean he ain't dead?"

"Isaiah, stop it!"

He sighed with an attitude. "Sorry, Mama. So what did he have to say for himself?"

"He wants a divorce." Hattie's heavy shoulders jerked up and down. She didn't think that she had any tears left, except once she actually said the word "divorce" aloud, she couldn't get them to stop.

The only thing that prevented Isaiah from saying exactly what was on his mind was the fact that his mother was bawling. Hattie had emotions of steel—"Cold as ice," as Rick James would say. But how mad could one person be when he witnessed his hero turning into mush? Isaiah was conflicted because he couldn't understand why she was so upset. He didn't know what to do or say. Isaiah really wanted to find his "father" and punch his lights out for hurting his mother again, but he couldn't do that. He wanted to cuss and let his mother know just how he really felt about the man, but he couldn't do that either. He decided to act on the one thing he could do. "I'm coming over."

"You don't have to do that. I'm all right. I just wanted you to know what was going on."

"I appreciate that, but I want to come see you."

"Isaiah, I'm fine."

"Mama—"

"I'm fine. Listen, I just felt that you should know. I've been 'round here crying long enough, but I'm through with that now."

Yup, same ole Mama, Isaiah thought.

"It stings a little, but I know I'll get through this. The good book says, 'My grace is sufficient for you, for my power is made perfect in weakness.' Corinthians 12:9."

"Of course you'll get through this. So is that all he had to say?"

"Well, I didn't actually talk to him. Some heffa dropped off these papers to me the other day. Says—"

Isaiah cut her off, pissed. "Papers? You mean he didn't actually call you or nothing? He just served you papers?"

"Yes, sir."

"What a coward!"

"Isaiah."

"No, Mama, hear me out. He has never given you anything you needed. No money, no support, and not even an explanation for leaving you—or us. He can at least give you that now after all these years. You deserve to know the truth. Am I right?"

"Wrong. I don't even want no explanation."

"What?" he questioned in disbelief.

"That's right. He doesn't owe me nothing."

"You crazy."

"Don't talk like that, boy. I raised you." They both stopped to ponder in silence. She noticed that the sun had gone down and darkness filled the room. Hattie flicked on the lamp next to her and took a deep breath. "Two more things and then I'll leave it alone. One, I'ma need you to book some tickets, cause we gotta go to 'Sippi and get this over with. And lastly, what I'm having trouble with the most is the fact that this is it. Not only will I be alone but I will also be a divorced woman. What would Jesus think about that being on my record?"

"That's not the worst you've done," he mumbled.

"Whatchu say?"

"Nothing." He shook his head at her sliding the travel arrangements in before getting off the phone. Isaiah wouldn't question her tonight, but would be all over her in the morning.

"Well, I'm through with it. I'ma do a little reading in my Bible before I turn in. Good night and behave yo' self. Hear me?" She slid her reading glasses on.

"Yes, Mama." *At least she's back to normal.* "Good night, wise woman."

They shared a laugh before disconnecting. She felt relief from finally talking to someone. Hattie had found out about the affair—better yet, she'd witnessed it—but never told her children. One thing that she was sure of: She would never shed another tear for Mr. Baker.

* * *

Ring. Ring. Hattie jolted out of her sleep. Her eyes began to focus and she refused to move until her head was entirely clear. The phone stopped ringing and she wondered why Christopher didn't catch it. Hattie swung her tree-trunk legs over the side of the bed and sat for a minute.

"Christopher?" Hattie paused and listened for any sounds of life. "Christopher," she shouted a little louder. "Boy, I know you hear me." She waited a few more seconds, then decided to go and check to make sure he was still breathing. *I can't have no dead people up in my house.*

Hattie stood and adjusted her lavender polka-dot nightgown and twisted headscarf. She looked down at the clock. It read eleven in angry red block numbers. She took a step and heard a voice, but couldn't place where it came from. She heard her name and actually thought that maybe Jesus was calling for her.

Hattie stretched her arms out to the sky and cried, "Lord Jesus. Is it my time already? I'm sorry for my ill thoughts about Wild Cat. I promise that I don't *really* want lightning to strike him dead. That was just a quick thought because he hurt me so. And I'm sorry about thinking Christopher was trying to steal from me. I do realize that some ex-cons really do get rehab—re—oh, you know what I'm trying to say." She then heard a longer mumble. She wasn't sure if Jesus was answering her or not, but either way, she couldn't comprehend it.

She took a couple of slow steps down the stairs and she heard it again. Hattie grabbed a glass from the table to use as a weapon, just in case, but felt silly when she realized that it was only Benjamin talking on her answering machine. She headed straight for the machine, but the message was complete. She took a deep breath and pressed play.

"Mae. Been a lon' time." Hattie rolled her eyes and sat down in her chair. "Just callin' to ask when you'll be in town. Court's in a couple days and I was hoping to talk to ya before then. I'm sure you got them papers by now." Hattie scrunched up her eyebrows and shook her head as if Benjamin could see her through the machine.

"Now, I hope that we can meet cord—, on good terms. I don't want no fussin' and fightin' now, just a good clean break, okay? Now, I'm 'bout to go get some rest. I 'spect you are too, so I'll just see you later. Night."

"A good clean break," huh? I hope he doesn't think that I still want him and gonna fight over him. She shook her head, unsure of how

she should take the message. Part of her wanted to strangle him for his egotistical thinking, and for her not wanting to legally let him go because of the simple fact that it would permanently close a major chapter in her life. A knot formed in the pit of her stomach.

Hattie mostly wanted to be done with all this and didn't want to be bothered. But to be honest, there was also a small part of her that wanted to see him, to see if he had changed any, but feared that she might fall in love again. Hattie wondered if Benjamin wanted to see her for that reason too.

Hattie shuffled by Christopher's door to find it open wide and dark. She turned on the light, curious to see if he had made any changes to his room since the last time she snooped through his stuff a few months ago. Hattie didn't think she would find anything in particular, but she was curious as to why he kept his door shut all the time. She looked both ways before tiptoeing in. The first thing Hattie noticed was clothes strewn all over the floor. *So that's why his door has been shut lately. He knew that I would be all over his head if I got wind of this mess! I'll just have to pretend that I never saw this. Somehow.*

Hattie walked further into the room, looking from side to side, making sure she didn't miss a thing. But suddenly she saw something that was different. It was definitely a color she had never seen inside Christopher's room before—pink and black. When she got closer, she nearly fainted.

"Condoms! What the hell is he doing with some condoms," Hattie screamed. She didn't care if Christopher walked in on her going through his things now. What she was concerned about was whether he was using these condoms in her house. She picked up the box from his nightstand; growled, crumpled it, and threw it down. She pounded on the box with her foot and looked on the nightstand for any more, but something else caught her eye.

Hattie leaned over to take a closer look at the picture that was taped to the wall. At first glance, she thought it was Christopher and a girlfriend. Once she looked again, she noticed that the woman looked too old to be young Christopher's girlfriend. *Guess he found another picture.* Hattie eased the picture off the wall and flipped it over. *Me and my boy at Granny's house. September 1990.*

That Juanita heffa. Christopher's mother. Hattie remembered when she met Christopher, he told her about his mother's lovely tattoo of a middle finger. And there it was on her right arm just as plain as day. Hattie sucked her teeth as she stared into the incompetent mother's eyes. But then she thought about it. *I'm no better than this woman. She abandoned her son when he got locked up, and I abandoned my Ruth Anne when she got knocked up.* Hattie tried to choke back her tears but was unsuccessful. She flopped down on Christopher's bed before hearing a car door slam.

Hattie jumped and scooted over to the wall to replace Christopher's picture, but forgot that Christopher had a waterbed. Every time she tried to move, the bed fought back. She got the picture reposted, but had a hard time getting out of the bed. The front door opened and shut quietly. Hattie gave up on getting out the bed peacefully and opted to roll out onto the floor. Boom!

"Grandma?" Christopher followed the noise into his own room. Hattie looked up just in time to see Christopher standing in the doorway.

"Hey, sugar. Home so early?"

*   *   *

The whole airport experience was a circus! From Hattie snapping off at the TSA agent for getting patted down, to her snacks being thrown away, to a bottle of juice being too expensive, to the seat numbers being too small to read, Hattie was ready to go back home. They almost missed their flight after the hell she raised at every checkpoint. Fearing they would be banned from the airport, Isaiah worked overtime to apologize to everyone Hattie interacted with. Christopher teetered between laughing and egging her on. Isaiah cursed his dad for putting him in this situation.

The family couldn't wait to get settled in at the hotel. Isaiah and Christopher shared a room to give Hattie her space. Isaiah kept Hattie's extra key, just in case. Out of sheer embarrassment and fatigue, Isaiah and Christopher opted for room service, and Hattie ordered in as well. Isaiah was hoping that after a good night's rest and returning to her hometown, his mother would simmer down some.

The next day, Isaiah went over to his mother's room to see if she was ready. After knocking a few times, Hattie called out to let himself in. After a few anxious minutes of patiently waiting, he let Christopher in, just in time for Hattie to wobble out of the bathroom adjusting her purple-striped church hat. She dug a little further into her suitcase and finally found what she was looking for—her black satin gloves.

"Mama. You're going to court, not church. You don't need all that."

"I'll go any way I please. Move." She swatted Isaiah out of the way. "You got them papers?"

"They in my purse." Hattie patted herself down, looking for something. She glanced over at the nightstand, table, and did a one-eighty in the middle of the floor. "Can one of you go grab my glasses?"

"Mama—" Isaiah tried to cut in.

"I can't find them anywhere."

Christopher tried to interject. "Grandma, they're—"

"And I swear I just had them."

Isaiah grabbed her shoulder, turning her to face him, and moved her glasses from her head to put them on her face. "All right then, let's roll."

Christopher tried to chuckle to himself discreetly, but got caught by Hattie's heavyweight purse when she swung it over her shoulder. "Bastard," Hattie mumbled. Christopher straightened up. Isaiah closed the door behind the family and they were off to finally close the Benjamin "Wild Cat" Baker chapter of their lives.

* * *

Instead of showing up fifteen minutes early per the court's request, the family showed up fifteen minutes *late* to the hearing after Hattie insisted they take a "shortcut" that led them to closed roads, construction, and a dead end. Isaiah should've known better than to take advice from someone who hadn't been in the area for decades. This minor setback naturally put Hattie in the best of moods. Not only did she cause a scene while walking up to the courthouse, but she also had to put on a show when she was asked to remove her hat, gloves, and purse to put them through the metal detector. Hattie claimed that one officer put their wand up her dress and "copped a feel" just like at the airport, which led to Isaiah reigniting his apology tour.

"I guess Benjamin still don't know how to tell time. He ain't even here and this was his idea."

Isaiah rolled his eyes. "Mama, he's not part of the greeting committee. They put him in one of the rooms in the back. We gotta follow him." He held his hands out to help Hattie up, but she swatted them away. Once she finally scooted and grunted her way off the hard bench, the officer escorted them down the quiet corridor to Room B. Officer Nunez rapped softly on the door. Before walking away, he showed Christopher the way to the restroom. A familiar face appeared inches away from Hattie once the door finally opened.

"Well, well. Look what the cat drug in." Benjamin laughed at his corny joke, and received crickets and daggers.

"Ya mama." Hattie snapped, pushing Benjamin out of the way with her purse. He whimpered when the blow hit him right in the gut.

Benjamin held out his hand to Isaiah. "Wow! This can't be my son."

Isaiah walked past Benjamin. "It's not." Benjamin solemnly shut the door and returned to his seat. Once Isaiah looked over and saw that a woman was seated next to Benjamin, he shook his head, knowing that Hattie would without a doubt go off. *This broom closet is not big enough for Mama, ole boy, and some other woman. I need to say a quick prayer*, Isaiah thought.

The third woman in the room stood from her place at the head of the table. "Good afternoon. I am the mediator assigned to your case, Katina Rawlins, and I will be facilitating this hearing." She leaned over and shook Hattie's and Isaiah's hands. They both introduced themselves and everyone took a seat. Hattie hoped the proceedings wouldn't take long, partly because the plain room was so utterly bleak. Obviously, the "decorator" didn't want anyone getting comfortable.

There was a small knock, and Christopher quietly backed into the room and closed the door. Once he turned around, his mouth dropped.

"Mama?" Christopher squinted.

"What?" Hattie asked, without turning.

The mystery woman rose out of her seat and spoke for the first time since Hattie entered the room. "My baby!" She held out her arms and waited for Christopher to come to her. He looked to Hattie, as if to ask for permission. Both Hattie and Isaiah looked confused and offered no help to Christopher. So he followed his instinct and hugged his biological mother.

Hattie spoke up. "So, you're that Juanita chick, huh?" *I thought she looked familiar.*

"Yeah. How you know?" Juanita, while holding on to Christopher, had turned her body so that Hattie could clearly see her tattoo.

"Lucky guess." Hattie sucked her teeth and sat back in her seat. Her lips were pursed so tight a coffee straw couldn't sneak through. *I'm gonna sit here and be good. Lord, please don't make them have to call the cops up in here. This heffa is sitting here givin' all of us the finger with that tacky tattoo. I mean, who does she think she is? Wait, I gotta say something. Just one thing, then I'll be good.* "So where the hell have you been for the last couple of years? You know your boy has been missing you and wondering where you were. Did you even know he went to juvie?"

Juanita let Christopher go and turned to face her challenger. "Of course I knew he was gone."

"So why didn't you get him? Where'd you expect him to stay?"

"I didn't know he was out. By the time I called up there, they said he already left. Why you asking so many questions about my business? And why do you have our son?"

"Our?" Hattie and Isaiah shouted. Isaiah stood and Hattie eventually made her way to her feet.

"Yeah, that's what I said."

"Wait, you don't mean biological. You mean 'our son' just cause y'all together, right?" Isaiah asked, hoping for the latter.

"No, biological," she stated quietly. Now all eyes were on her. Apparently, she was the only one who'd been privy to that information. Benjamin looked at Juanita like she had grown another head.

Benjamin's eyes pleaded with her. "Why didn't you tell me he was mine?" He stood to face her.

Juanita looked down at her fingernails. "Well, we were broken up at the time and I moved away for a bit."

"And?"

"There is no *and*," she shot back, getting the bass back in her voice. "Besides, you couldn't even take care of your own kids, so I figured that you probably wouldn't take care of mine." Benjamin flopped down in his chair and held his head down in his hands. "I was too young to care for him at the time, so he spent most of his time with his auntie. Now why *she* didn't get him when he got out is beyond me."

Christopher looked completely defeated. He'd finally heard the truth about his father. His mother always told him that his father didn't want him, but there was a vast difference between "doesn't want" and "doesn't know." *I can't believe her! How could she do this to me? I can't even look at her right now*, Christopher thought. He clenched his fists and a couple of unwanted tears escaped his eyes. He picked up a chair and set it down in the furthest corner away from everybody.

Hattie attempted to go over to comfort Christopher, but Isaiah grabbed her arm. "Give him some space." Hattie and Isaiah sat back down. He planted his arm around his mother. She rocked in her chair and silently cried for Christopher.

Juanita looked at all the people in the room; at all the people who refused to look at her and held expressions full of either rage, pity, or simply sadness. "What?" she said to no one in particular, and received no response.

Mediator Rawlins intervened. "I'm sorry. I realize that this is a very delicate time now for your families, but we have to move forward with the divorce proceedings. Are both parties in agreement?" Hattie and Benjamin nodded and they continued with their original plan.

*   *   *

"So I guess that's it," Benjamin gave a lame attempt to engage in conversation after Mediator Rawlins exited. They learned that they'd have one more hearing before they'd be officially divorced. They both looked forward to putting this legal stuff behind them.

"Yup," Hattie fiddled with her purse and wouldn't look at Benjamin. He stared at her, looking for the right words. He knew that the wrong ones would spark her mean streak, and he also knew that he would be outnumbered with Isaiah in the mix.

"Wait for me in the car," Benjamin mumbled to Juanita. She made a stank face but reluctantly left the room. She snuck a peek at Christopher, who still hadn't budged, and kept on walking. Benjamin turned his chair to face Hattie. "I have done a lot of bad things to the people in this room."

"You got that right," Isaiah cut in. Benjamin looked at him before focusing back on Hattie.

"And I'm man enough to admit that, but I would like to take this time to right my wrongs." He stopped to gauge her response.

"Go on." She still hadn't given the eye contact and attention that Benjamin was hoping for, but the fact that she responded at all was a start.

"I was hoping to say this in private, but, I apolo—no, I am deeply sorry for hurting you all them years ago and leaving you to raise our kids on your own. You didn't deserve it, and I realize I can never repay you. I was in a totally different place then than I am now."

"Well, it's too late to run that garbage on the fact that you were too young to have a child and all that," Isaiah retorted. "I didn't ask to be born."

"You have no idea whatchu talkin' bout, son."

"Don't call me that."

"Well, whether you like it or not, I am still your father."

"You are my *dad*, but not by choice. A father is a person who takes care of their responsibilities and raises their children. You ain't nobody's father." Isaiah stood with his fists clenched.

"That's not what Lisa tells me every weekend." Benjamin stood. Now he had Hattie's attention.

"Whatchu talkin' about, Benjamin?"

"Lisa came to live with me shortly after you kicked her out."

"How—"

"She looked me up and begged me to help her out. Said you didn't want 'pregnant heathens' in your house. So, I signed her out of that shit shack you put her in and brought her back to 'Sippi with me." Hattie's body jerked as she cried like a baby. She'd lost touch with her daughter after putting her in a teen mothers' center. She hated herself for doing that, but she didn't want to condone her daughter's behavior. Hattie didn't want her church friends to think that she hadn't raised her right, but she realized that after all these years of missing her and not even laying an eye on her only grandchild, it shouldn't have mattered what anybody else thought. Hattie should've supported her. "So what I'm saying is, Isaiah, I may have been nothing to you, but I'm err'thang to her. I'm sorry that it happened that way, and if I could do it all again, I definitely would change some thangs, but I can't."

"Where is Ruth Anne now?" Hattie asked.

"Mae, she goes by Lisa. She's in Virginia, married. Got another kid. This one's a girl. One of each." He smiled as he fished out his wallet and pulled out a recent family photo. Benjamin handed it to Hattie. Isaiah sat down and looked over his mother's shoulder. She flipped the picture over and read Lisa's caption. *Me, Simon, Brandon (a handsome twenty-one), and Gerri (a sassy mini-me at sixteen). Love you, Daddy. Come visit again soon!*

A knife pierced Hattie's heart. Hattie had never received an invitation to see her daughter. In fact, it wasn't until today that she'd heard Lisa had a boy as her first child, much less had another one. And married? "I'm no different from Juanita."

"Yes you are, Mama," Isaiah quickly spoke up.

"No, listen. I abandoned Ruth Anne—Lisa, or whatever you want to call her—just like Juanita abandoned Christopher. I can't fix the past either, but I for damn sure don't want to stay living in it." She let out a heavy sigh. "We all have some growin' up to do and it shouldn't involve hate. Life is too short for us to be hating each other like we do. I have missed over twenty years of this child's life." Hattie gripped the picture as she preached, but let it go slightly for fear of crumpling it. "I can't miss another twenty without my daughter. And, Benjamin, you've missed all twenty of Christopher's years and almost forty of Isaiah's. It's time for some catchin' up. We've all got work to do. Come here, Christopher."

Hattie held out her hand. Christopher sauntered over to the group and stood closer to her than to Benjamin. "Christopher, you heard what I said about hate, right?" His face never let go of his frown, but forced out a "Yes" to make his grandma happy. "Now, I know you're angry; we all are for all kinds of reasons, but I need you to know that it's not this man's fault. If what yo mama said was true, you can't be angry with him."

"But *you* shouldn't be telling me this; my mama should," Christopher spat.

"I know, baby. That's true. But I'm trying to do what's right for your sake. This is Benjamin Baker, and Benjamin, this is Christopher Atkins." Hattie made the men shake.

"How did y'all end up together?" Benjamin questioned.

"Long story." Hattie wasn't in the storytelling mood.

"So, Benjamin." Isaiah said, and Hattie froze. She never heard her son call him by his first name. Usually it was "that clown," "your ex," "him," or "sperm donor," depending on how spiteful he was feeling. "What made you up and leave us if it wasn't because of your age, and why do all this now? Mama may not want answers, but I do."

Benjamin breathed deeply before speaking. "I was immature, dumb, and wasn't ready to settle down. Yeah, I loved your mother, and I loved my children, but I wasn't focused on the future. I was focused on only myself. I ended up getting engaged to two women after your mother. Woman named Tanisha, and Juanita. Me and Tanisha were together for years but I couldn't, you know, seal the deal. Not legally, of course, and I really wasn't ready to do that anyway. She left me, and then I got with Juanita. We've been on and off for years. I knew she had a kid, but that was the extent of it. I recently asked her to marry me, and I mean, she was really holding me to it, too. Then I had to fess up that I was still married. So, she was the one who got things rolling. Despite what happened today, I'm glad all y'all are here. I really needed y'all to see how sorry I am for all the harm I've caused now and over the years. I'm willing to do whatever it takes to fix the broken relationships between us, sons." He looked from Isaiah to Christopher and back several times waiting for a response.

"It'll take some time, man. I can't make any promises," Isaiah spoke first.

"Yeah," Christopher seconded.

"All I want is for you fellas to think about it. Look, I'll give you my card. It's got my cell number on there. Call your ole mane up anytime you want." He dug in his pants back pocket and pulled out his wallet again, but fingered a different compartment. Benjamin pulled out three business cards and handed them out to his family. He was relieved that everyone accepted them. "I gotta go now. Gotta drop her off and go to work in a few. Christopher," he gathered his thoughts before continuing. "I really hope that we can build something, mane. Call me." Benjamin patted Christopher on his shoulder. "Mae, Isaiah, keep in touch."

"Wait! Don't they have another sister or brother?" Hattie inquired. Benjamin looked dumbfounded. Isaiah was highly confused, and she refused to look at him for fear that he would ask for an explanation before she received the truth. Hattie got up and moved closer to him. "The year you left, I saw you walking down the street from the corner store with your hand on some woman's pregnant belly. What happened with that?"

"Stillborn," he answered quietly. No one said a word. "Gimme a call, okay." He left without waiting for a response, just in time to hear Juanita hollering at him down the hallway for taking so long.

Hattie sighed. She didn't expect to hear all that and didn't know how to respond, so she just kept it moving. However, she did realize that she had some explaining to do once they got into the car. "You boys ready?" The family slowly walked to the door without speaking. Christopher stopped at the door. Hattie couldn't see what he was doing behind her back, but she could definitely hear the sound of a rip. She didn't know whether to laugh, yell, or cry, but she waited for Christopher to catch up to her. She wrapped her arm around him and kissed him on the cheek. And for once, he didn't wipe it off.

Mousetrap

Dear children, let us not love with words or tongue but with actions and in truth. (I John 3:18)

Isaiah opened the front door and immediately grew suspicious. The stale aroma informed him that nothing had been cooked or baked all day. The only reason neither he nor Christopher, who was behind him, didn't rush in to look for a corpse was because they heard giggling. Isaiah and Christopher exchanged confused looks as they followed the girly laughs. As the men entered the family room, they found Hattie lying across the floor, twirling her wig with her finger, and swinging her legs in the air like an eight-year-old. She didn't bother to break her phone conversation until Isaiah spoke.

"What the hell is going on in here?"

The cordless phone tumbled out of Hattie's hand. "Oh shit! You scared me." She picked up the phone and told the person on the line that she'd call them back later. Hattie looked up at her boys. "When you get here and why are you cussin' in my house?" She slammed her hand on the carpet for emphasis. Now this was the lady they knew and loved.

"We just got here. And why are you sittin' up here lookin' like some lil ole school girl, cussin' and carrying on? I wanna know what happened to my mama."

"Yeah. And, who were you talking to?" Christopher added. Isaiah shook his head in silence. Hattie glared at Christopher. If she were on her feet, she would've popped him good. *Nobody questions Hattie Mae Atkins.*

"Help me up." Hattie rolled over and stretched her arms out, and together the men dragged her to her feet. Since her divorce a year ago, she had lost a little over forty pounds. She still had at least one hundred more to go, but who was counting. With her new weight loss, she appeared a bit cockier—putting an extra wiggle in her step and wearing a darker wig, in contrast to her usual salt and pepper one. Isaiah loved his mother's newfound confidence in herself, but it sickened him to imagine that she was attempting to get her "groove" back. One thing that hadn't changed was her heavy limp. Isaiah smiled as she hobbled past him.

"I might go to Jackson."

Isaiah's smile vanished. "Wait, what? Now?"

"No, fool. Next weekend."

"Whatchu going there for?" Christopher piped in.

"And how are you getting there?"

"Might be flying." Hattie left the room with her boys right on her heels.

"You don't even like planes! You call them flying death traps. And, after that performance you put on last time, you're probably on the No Fly List. Who you going with?"

"I'm going by myself. I don't need no chaperone. I'm grown."

"Okay, Ms. Grown. Remember the last time you took a trip without me? You left with a suitcase and a duffel bag you like to call a purse, but came back with only the dress you had on, a crooked wig, and this knucklehead," he said, crooking a thumb at Christopher. Isaiah grew tired of his mother's stubbornness; in his forty-three years on earth, he never said anything that made her change her tune.

"Oh, hush," Hattie waved him off.

"Aren't you gonna answer Chris? He raised a good question. Why are you going?" He grabbed his mother by the shoulders to keep her from walking away.

She huffed. "I'm just visiting a friend, that's all. Leave me alone. Don't y'all have somethin' to do?" Then she made the pricey mistake in mumbling, "He don't put me on the witness stand like this."

Isaiah hit the ceiling. "He! Who the hell is *he*? You got a man?" Just saying the word *man* left a foul taste in his mouth. The three went back and forth, getting no closer to the truth with each question. The interrogation led Hattie to shut down and go to her room. He knew she could handle herself, but his mother hadn't dated anyone since his father and was never this secretive. He had to get to the bottom of this before next Thursday afternoon, the day of her "maybe" departure.

* * *

"What am I supposed to do with this?" Hattie turned the phone on all sides to analyze the new device.

"It's a cell phone. Remember, you gotta keep it charged so you can talk on it," Isaiah explained. He bought one from the wireless store where Christopher was working to pay for his college tuition. Christopher couldn't afford to live on his own yet, but as soon as he saved up enough, he would be out of Hattie's house. And he couldn't wait!

"I don't know why y'all bought me this fancy thing, knowing that I don't know a damn thing about it."

"Trust me, it ain't fancy," Christopher remarked. Isaiah elbowed Christopher and shot him a look.

"I'm trying to say that we picked out the most basic phone for you. You probably can't even text on it." Christopher's reassuring comment was met with one blank and one annoyed stare.

Hattie looked to Isaiah. "What is he saying?"

"Don't even worry about it. We gotta go." Isaiah still didn't approve of her field trip, but how could he stop her? He hated the fact that she was going to meet some strange guy in another state. She got a free trip out of it, but he had far too many questions: Where did he come from, what does he do, has he ever killed anyone before? You know, the basics. But like she said, she was no child.

Hattie turned to give Christopher a hug and kiss while lecturing him about not having wild orgies in her house. She explained she had seen the show *Real Sex* before ("accidentally") and knew what happened when a bunch of people from the opposite sex gathered with no supervision. She'd met a couple of his friends once or twice before, and if she'd been given advance notice, she would've locked up her silver. Hattie snatched up her Bible and headed out.

On the way to the airport, Isaiah attempted to explain how Hattie's new cell phone worked, beginning with the on/off button. He ended up getting so frustrated that he told her to just leave the phone on and to push one button—the green answer button. He would hang up first so she didn't have to bother with ending the call. Hattie appeared to be satisfied with that simple task.

Once they reached the airport, Isaiah grabbed the closest skycap to help guide Hattie on where to go and what to do. She had never been on an airplane by herself, so he was trying to do all he could to prevent seeing her on the news standing in the middle of the airport screaming, with security assuming that she was a terrorist. Skycap Michael was nice enough; he not only took her suitcase, he helped her onto the curb and held onto her like a child. Isaiah just knew she was going to go off on him for his delicate treatment, but she played along. Even cracked a smile. Isaiah was puzzled by the positive changes in his mother, but instead of questioning her, he got back in his car once they disappeared inside.

* * *

The flight to Mississippi was a smooth one after Hattie fell asleep, though she created quite the scene before that. She hollered, literally, about being claustrophobic, and refused to sit in her assigned middle seat. The flight attendants had to change her seat twice, once to an aisle seat (until she complained about strangers' behinds bumping her shoulder and having no room to stretch her long chubby legs), and then to a window seat in an exit row. She really piped down when the pilot sent her a complimentary stiff drink. Other coach passengers appeared envious, but understood and probably would've chipped in to provide additional drinks. Hattie mistook the rum and a hint of Coke for straight Coke and downed it. New to the "worldly" side of hard liquor, within ten minutes, the heavyweight was down for the count for the rest of the flight.

Back on the ground, Hattie wheeled her suitcase to the pickup area and shuffled outside to wait for her ride. Clarence told her he would be in a burgundy Eldorado. She noticed a car slowly approaching her and bent down to peer through the window. The car came to a complete stop in front of her and parked. Next, a mocha-colored man leisurely stepped out from behind the wheel. He smiled, and she returned it.

"There's my brown sugar." The man walked around to the other side of the car, held out his arms for an embrace, and she went to him.

"My dumplin'." She could smell his cologne—Jovan Musk. It danced in her nostrils. Clarence kissed her sweaty cheek. The seventy-degree weather was a vast difference from the forty-degree weather she just left. She felt like she was going through the change all over again.

Clarence Brown was a friend of one of her high school girlfriends, Brandi, who thought that they should meet. Brandi's original plan was to introduce them through Skype; however, as electronically illiterate as Hattie was, she immediately shot down the idea. Instead, their romance began with a three-way call initiated by Brandi.

*   *   *

"Okay, Hattie. I need you to be on your best behavior. He's a nice guy; a God-fearing man, just like you like 'em. Except for that ex of yours."

Hattie laughed. "Girl, don't get me started on him. And this one better be cute. I know you like them insect-looking ones."

"What? All my men look good," Brandi growled.

"What about Spider James? When the lights went out, you couldn't see him, but it felt like he had about eight hands touchin' all the right spots at the same time! Isn't that what you said?" The women shared a laugh, then got down to business.

"All right now, remember what I told you."

"I forgot already."

"Behave!" Before Hattie could respond, Brandi clicked over.

Once she heard another click, Hattie started in. "You better not have hooked me up with Spider James's brother, neither."

"Thankfully, I'm the only child," a man responded.

Hattie covered her mouth. "Oops, I'm sorry. I was just messin' with Brandi." The man laughed. *At least he's got a sense of humor. Definitely a bonus.*

"It's nice to finally meet you, Ms. Hattie Mae. Our friend here has talked about you for quite some time now."

"Nice to meet you too, Clarence." Hattie was scared to say too much more for fear of ruining their phone date. Her last date had been in the sixties, so she was beyond rusty.

"So, are you originally from Jackson?"

"Born and raised. Left in '73."

"Oh, okay. So you're no stranger to Pineapple Grill and Big Key Inn."

"Pineapple is my favorite spot! Nobody can throw down in the kitchen like Shirley. I tried to steal her recipes back in the day, but my greens and cornbread always tasted a *tad* bit different. Shoot, maybe even better, but don't tell Big Shirl!" Everybody laughed, then Brandi spoke up.

"Well, it sounds like y'all are getting along just fine. So I'ma get off of here and talk to y'all later." She hung up and disconnected everyone. Hattie yelled out every cuss word in the book until the phone rang a few minutes later.

"I'd love to sample your greens and cornbread sometime to judge which is better," Clarence stated matter-of-factly. Hattie beamed.

*   *   *

Hattie's boys had been left totally in the dark about her eight-month romance. With Christopher away at class, out with his friends, or at work, Hattie could do whatever she wanted before 10 p.m., when he usually returned home. Occasionally, she and Clarence would talk well into the night; those were the nights she would stay in her room with the door closed. Sometimes those long nights would be on Saturday, and she would either show up late to church or doze off during service. Pastor Stanley caught her snoring one time, because she sat almost under his nose. He hadn't let her live that down since. She told Clarence that they'd have to cut down on their Saturday night rendezvous.

Although she was falling hard for this man, this weekend would be the first time they'd see each other in person. Sure, they'd exchanged pictures, but that was the extent of it, and the reason she hadn't fallen completely for him. *What if the pictures were old? What if they weren't really him? What if that sexy voice doesn't match?*

When she finally saw Clarence for the first time, it put her over the edge. His pictures did him *no* justice. She loved his deep dimples and honest eyes. He even put the nail in the coffin by showing up in a caramel suit, topped with a Paddington Bear-looking hat. Clarence caught her staring at him and he smiled.

"Let's get out of here." He grabbed Hattie's suitcase and loaded it into the trunk after he opened the door for her. She flopped down in the seat, and it was his turn to give her a once-over. He licked his lips and grinned. Hattie caught Clarence out of the corner of her eye. *I love this dirty old man!*

Clarence had invited Hattie there to accompany him to a wedding. One of his best friends was getting married and he "wanted his lady there." He placed a double whammy on her by including Sunday brunch with his children on the itinerary. Hattie wasn't thrilled about the additional plans, but she guessed it was necessary if they were to continue dating and perhaps more.

The couple engaged in casual conversation on the way to Clarence's house. Once inside, he wheeled Hattie's luggage into his guest bedroom. He left her alone in the room to nap and get herself situated. She felt like she'd pushed the plane there instead of riding on it. The four-hour trip left Hattie exhausted. Clarence snuck out while she was sleeping to pick up dinner. When Sleeping Beauty awakened, they ate with the television on low and retired to their rooms for the night. It was at that point that she caught sight of the stunning tulips on the dresser and the fragrant potpourri that brought her a sense of calm.

The next morning, Clarence had to work for a few hours at the bank, although he had requested to leave early. His supervisor was shocked due to Clarence's perfect attendance record, but knew the reasoning behind his request must have been extremely important.

First, Clarence dropped Hattie off at the mall. She refused to stay idle at his place and wait for him to get off work. Besides her quick divorce trip, Hattie hadn't been back home to Jackson in years, so she planned to get out some. The movie theater was right by the mall, so she would have plenty to do. Besides, she wasn't sure if the dress she'd brought with her for tomorrow was stylish enough. She hated shopping, but desperately needed to upgrade her wardrobe. Brandi said she would help her pick out an outfit, but could only meet her after work. Hattie didn't have that kind of time, so she decided to get a head start.

She looked around her hometown from where she was standing and took it all in while waiting for the mall to open. She couldn't believe how much it had changed. Her eyes moistened. She couldn't possibly be homesick after thirty-plus years, could she? She didn't regret uprooting her family to move to a brand-new state, did she? Hattie had every right to want a change in scenery after her husband abandoned her. It was his fault she no longer felt at home here.

Once the mall doors opened, Hattie and a few others filed in. Hattie wandered around the mall, amazed and overwhelmed at the variety of stores. This mall wasn't even here when she left. She solemnly shook her head and continued walking. Hattie took a couple of brief breaks, but finally ended up in one of her favorite stores of all time—JCPenney. She loved how their "one-day sale" lasted all week and the next. They also carried a wide variety of women's fashions. *Not every dress my size has to look like a tent!*

Hattie grabbed one lady folding basic tees to help her find a dress. Almost everything the lady pulled out Hattie shook her head at. After three noes, Catherine finally asked her *specifically* what she was looking for.

"I told you, I gotta find a dress."

The woman rolled her eyes. "I know, but what *kind* of dress? I've been pulling out dresses, but you don't like them. What do you need it for? Casual, a party, a special event—"

"That's right! I gotta go to a wedding."

"Now we're getting somewhere! Let's step over to our Special Occasion section." The two women went through the same process; Catherine would pull out options and Hattie would shoot them down. Eventually, the saleslady fussed with her for not trying anything on. Hattie tried the next selection that was handed to her and found it was the perfect match for her. Catherine cheered and guided Hattie toward the checkout line, but Hattie stopped in her tracks.

"Uh-un. I ain't done yet. I gotta find something for Sunday dinner. Come on." Catherine's mouth dropped and she quickly blurted out that she was past due for her break. She flew in the other direction; Hattie overheard her telling a coworker to steer clear of the dress section and that she was going on a much-needed smoke break.

Tired from all the walking and carrying her dress bag around, Hattie walked over to the movie theater. The last time she was in one, *Sister Act* may have been playing. Her children liked to go in groups with their friends, especially her daughter, Ruth Anne. Hattie suspected that she and her little fast-tailed girlfriends liked to meet up with boys there. She never asked her which one of them knocked her up at seventeen. Tears brimmed in her eyes as she recalled the last conversation with her. Hattie would give anything to talk to her, see her smile, or take her to the movies again.

Hattie took a deep breath and wiped the tears on the back of her hand as she stepped into the theater. Grateful she didn't have to walk far, she settled on a movie that started in fifteen minutes and starred Denzel Washington—her all-time favorite actor. *Can't go wrong with Mr. Washington!* Hattie tried her best to squeeze into one of the back seats. *This is why I don't come to these damn places! Not fit for pleasantly plump people. I should sue 'em.*

Hattie carried on a whole conversation with herself for several minutes until she heard another guest arrive. The woman's high-pitched laugh echoed around the room, which immediately annoyed Hattie. She was draping herself over her man, almost as if she were drunk. Hattie sucked her teeth in disgust. The woman let go of the man only to shuffle through the aisle, three rows in front of Hattie, to choose a seat. The man slapped her on her backside, causing yet another annoying giggle.

Something other than what was coming out of the woman's mouth bothered her. She had a familiar look to her, but Hattie couldn't place her. Archnemesis? Old neighbor's daughter? It irritated her like a piece of corn stuck in her teeth. Then it hit her before the theater went black. How many Black women had a middle finger tattooed on their arm? None other than the wannabe diva Juanita

Atkins: Christopher's mother and Benjamin's fiancée. Or at least she *thought* they were still engaged. Judging by the way she held on to this mystery man and allowed him to grope her in places Hattie couldn't even find after all these years, she guessed that Juanita and Benjamin wouldn't be together much longer.

As if on cue, the couple leaned in for a long noisy smooch, which made Hattie's stomach churn. Even though Benjamin had cheated on her, she couldn't let him get played like this. She felt a sense of obligation to him, though she didn't understand why. Once the movie finally began, she wound up watching Juanita more than Denzel, which pissed her off. Hattie gritted her teeth. She couldn't wait to talk to Benjamin.

One of those annoying cellphone ringtones broke Hattie's concentration. At first she thought Juanita was ignoring hers, but when she didn't stop pushing up on her date and everyone else in the theater was too far from her, process of elimination told her to check her own. Once she finally dug the irritating contraption out of her purse, she'd missed the call. Luckily, Isaiah called her right back.

"Hey Mama. How's everything going?"

"Fine. I need you to do me a favor."

"I'm good too, thanks for asking."

"Oh hush, boy."

"What's all that noise in the background?"

"I'm at the movies." Juanita's lover turned around and shushed her. "No, you shh! Gon' tell me. You missin' the movie anyway bein' all hugged up." She had to stop herself. Juanita turned around. Hoping that she wouldn't be able to see in the dark, Hattie shielded her face and went back to her conversation with Isaiah. "I need you to give me a number," she whispered.

"Six," he laughed at his lame joke. Hattie wasn't enthused. "I'm just playing. Whatchu need?"

"I need you to find your daddy's number." She was met with silence. "Hello—"

"What the hell is going on that you gotta call him? You need me to come down there? I've got a couple of vacation days saved up."

"No! I just need to tell him something. Something important."

"Some man that Clarence is, driving you back to your ex-husband. I mean, damn."

"Just give me the damn number," Hattie was no longer whispering and had caught the attention of the patrons on the other side of the theater. She calmed herself down and tried to speak quieter. "I really need to speak to him right quick. Can you *please* give me his number, or have him call me?"

Isaiah huffed. "I threw it away."

"Why?"

"Are you serious? I didn't even have it for five minutes." He sighed. Isaiah didn't know why his mother was being so secretive again, but he knew that if she really wanted it, it had to be for a good reason. He didn't push—yet. "Tell ya what. I will look him up and call you back with his number."

"Oh thank you, baby!"

"IF—you tell me why." They went back and forth for another minute until they reached a consensus. Hattie would explain after she talked to Benjamin. She feared that if he knew the reason beforehand, he would try to talk her out of doing what she had planned. Isaiah called back twenty minutes after the movie ended and instructed her again on how to use the phone. The theater was cleared out and Hattie made her move.

"Yell-ow?"

"Benjamin?"

"Mae. How you doin', sunshine?" She could tell he was grinning. He definitely must be in a good mood to call her pet names, since the last time they saw each other, they were ending their marriage.

"Just fine, and you?"

"Shocked as all get out to hear from you, but otherwise, I'm okay. I know you're not calling to wish me an early Happy Father's Day, so what's on your mind?"

Hattie took a deep breath. She hadn't rehearsed how she would break the news, but on the other hand, she wasn't the kind of lady to beat around the bush either. "Juanita's cheatin' on you. I just saw her." She silently scolded herself for her blunt ways, but she couldn't help herself. The silence on the other end made her feel a tinge of guilt. "Hello?"

"I'm here," Benjamin grunted. "You really can't get over me, can you? And you can't get over the fact that I'm 'bout to marry somebody else in a few weeks."

Hattie rolled her eyes. "I got a man. I ain't thinkin' 'bout you."

"What man?"

"I didn't call you to talk about me. Did you hear what I said?"

"Nita ain't cheatin'. Where would you get a story like that?"

"I just saw her. Clean out your ears, man!"

This caught his attention. "Saw her where? This should be good. She doesn't like to fly, so there's no way she—"

"In West Park movie theater, or whatever this is called. Park somethin'."

He took a minute to process what she was saying. "You're here," Benjamin shrieked. "For how long?"

"Focus. She was all hugged up with some man and swappin' lots of saliva."

He sighed. "That couldn't be her. She's at work."

"She's got a short blue or purple dress on. Sound familiar?"

Benjamin grew quiet. Hattie heard a door slam and a woman's voice in the background. "You have the wrong number; don't call here again." Silence. *That went better than I expected. Well, I hope he will wise up and give it to her good!*

Hattie finally rose from her seat and walked back to the mall entrance where she was dropped off. She was almost late to meet her man.

* * *

The wedding went off effortlessly. Beautiful church wedding, lovely reception. Hattie had never seen so much red and chocolate combinations in her life. Red tablecloths, red flowers, brown chair covers, chocolate candy—just too much. One thing for sure, she hadn't had that much fun in her life! Clarence got her up to dance, he introduced her to everyone he knew, and she smiled—that's what she missed the most. Smiling. When she was at home, it seemed as if all she ever did was fuss and frown. It was nice to be carefree for once.

Clarence and Hattie got up to dance again once Earth, Wind & Fire came on.

"Have I told you how stunning you look tonight, Ms. Atkins?"

"Yes you have, Mr. Brown. You look pretty handsome yourself."

"Thank you. Are you enjoying yourself?"

"Yes, very much so."

"Well, that makes me happy. I am too. Everyone adores you, like I do."

"Good." He then dipped her and planted a kiss on her lips. Her stomach tingled. Right before he brought her back up, she saw a familiar face walk through the entry doors. She stood up on her own and whipped her head.

"What's wrong, suga?"

Her eyes followed Benjamin into the room until his gaze caught hers. She spun back to Clarence. "My ex-husband is here." Her heart felt like it would jump right out and smack her in the face.

"Oh, I see." He loosened his embrace, but looked her in the eye. "Do you need a minute? I mean, do you still have feelings for this man?"

"No. He left me a long time ago and I've had *many* years to get over him. The only feeling I have for him is pity cause his woman is cheating on him. But then again, he did the same to me. So—"

"How do you know she's cheating?"

Hattie shook her head. "It's a long story."

"Would you like to leave, or—"

"Yes." They turned to leave when Benjamin appeared in front of them. "Benjamin. What are you doing here?"

"Hello there, Mae. I happen to know the bride pretty well."

"I'm sure you do," Hattie mumbled. Before she could introduce her beau, Clarence stepped next to her and introduced himself. "Well, now that you've been acquainted, we were just on our way out." She grabbed Clarence's arm, but Benjamin caught her by the shoulder.

"I need to talk to you for a minute, Mae. If you don't mind, Clarence."

Clarence narrowed his eyes, but instead of answering, he looked to Hattie to see what she wanted to do. She agreed to listen, but still clung onto Clarence. Benjamin didn't look pleased, but he spoke his piece anyway.

"Okay. Well, for starters, you were right. I confronted Juanita about what you told me."

"You saw him," Clarence questioned. He faced Hattie with a faint look of betrayal in his eyes.

Benjamin answered for her. "Called." Clarence's jaw tightened. "But, in her defense, she was only saving me from making the biggest mistake of my life. Stay cool, mane. We don't talk at all, but she called about this and I just want to thank you for that." He turned back to Hattie and wouldn't look away.

Hattie looked back and forth between the two men, wishing she could read Clarence's mind. She still had to go home with this man and spend two more nights with him, and here Benjamin was announcing to the world that she was calling him. Her palms grew sweaty. She didn't react well in tense situations, especially when she was in the hot seat. Luckily, Benjamin continued talking before she was forced to speak and say the wrong thing.

"I had to step out earlier. Too bad I came in so late. I'd just like to say that you're looking so beautiful tonight, Mae."

"Yes she is," Clarence drew her in close with his arm around her waist. "She—"

Benjamin cut in. "And I'd like to give us another shot."

Still Waters

Bear with each other and forgive whatever grievances you may have against one another. Forgive as the Lord forgave you. (Colossians 3:13)

"Don't come 'cause I asked you to. Come 'cause you'll get a chance to meet your family," Benjamin's husky voice brought Hattie pleasant memories from when their marriage was good. Now that they were divorced, he was calling her more than when they were courting.

Clarence coughed loudly, signaling that he was in the room. He had been visiting for the holiday weekend. Naturally, he was over during one of Wild Cat's calls, which was an instant trigger for him. Hattie looked at him and sighed heavily. "I'll think about it. I can't believe she's married and got two lil ones now."

"They ain't been little for a long time; Brandon's twenty-two and Gerri's seventeen."

Hattie flopped on the bed and peeked over her shoulder at her beau. "I'll let you know. Maybe I can get Clarence and the boys to come along."

"I'd love to see my boys. I don't know about that other sucka." Hattie sucked her teeth. "He ain't family."

"He might be soon."

"What! He proposed?" Benjamin's loud voice caught Clarence's attention.

"I might have," Clarence shouted back toward the phone.

Hattie shook her head. It was getting to be too much. "I'm going to bed. Good night, Benjamin."

"I wasn't done, Mae."

"The lady said good night," Clarence answered. Hattie tried to push Clarence back down onto the bed before the men started arguing—again. They had almost come to blows six months ago when they were in the same room. Ruined the end of the newly married couple's reception.

"I wasn't talking to you, you ole goat," Benjamin snapped. Before Clarence could fire back, Hattie quickly muttered a "bye" and hung up.

"What did he want this time?"

Solemnly, she stated, "Didn't you hear everything, you ole busybody? Well, it's my baby's fortieth birthday coming up. Her husband's throwing a surprise party for her, and I've been invited. I've never met him before, nor my grandbabies. These are my only grandbabies, you know."

"Oh, that would be nice. Tell me again why you've never met them?"

"I told you that I haven't talked to Ruth Anne, or Lisa, as she prefers to be called now, in over twenty years."

"But why?"

Hattie's sadness turned to irritation. "Go on to sleep, you ole goat. You asking too many questions, as late as it is." She turned off the light and angrily plopped down under the covers, turning her back to Clarence. Offended, Clarence closed his mouth and put his back to hers. His lips were shut tight, until a few minutes later when they parted to release his snores. Hattie quietly cried herself to sleep.

The next morning, Isaiah stopped by for breakfast, as he'd done every time Clarence was visiting. He still couldn't adjust to Hattie being in a relationship. This was her first since his father left and it was his job not to like the man. Since he didn't even like his own father, he'd give a hard time to *any* man she brought around.

This morning was different, Isaiah noticed. Neither of them was talking to the other; they only occasionally exchanged grunts. He smiled, wondering how much longer her suitor would last. He decided he would first stir the pot.

"Mama, why are you so quiet? Clarence got your tongue?" Isaiah scooped a fork full of scrambled eggs into his mouth. *And go!*

The couple looked at him; Hattie rolled her eyes and Clarence glared. "Just lost in my own thoughts, that's all."

"About what? About your little proposal?" Clarence questioned.

Isaiah choked, throwing him into a coughing fit. "What proposal? You proposed without my permission?"

"No, boy." Hattie waved Isaiah off. "This was my business to tell when I was ready," Hattie scolded Clarence, who took a wicked bite of his toast and turned around. Isaiah continued to look at his mother for answers.

"What's going on, Mama?"

"Your father invited us—"

"Thought you said Lisa's husband invited you," Clarence interrupted.

Now it was Hattie's turn to glare. "As I was saying, your father invited us to Ruth Anne's birthday party."

"Does she want you there?"

"That's the thing. It's a surprise party. She don't even know we were invited." Isaiah's face stared blankly, and for once, Hattie wasn't able to read his expression.

"I say we go down there and be the surprise. Wouldn't that be something? Just hop out the cake on they ass!" Clarence chuckled. Once he realized he was the only one laughing, he grabbed his coffee and left the room.

Hattie took a seat and looked her son in the eye. "What's on your mind, son?"

"Where you find that country bumpkin?" They both laughed.

"I heard that," Clarence yelled from the family room.

"Turn your hearing aid down," Hattie shouted. She'd never gone back and forth this much with Clarence like this before yesterday. She wondered if it was because of Benjamin or if this was what the future held.

Isaiah sighed. "I'm fine with going. It would be nice to see Lisa and meet my niece and nephew."

"But?"

"You know me so well, Mama. But, I don't want to crash LeeLee'sparty. It would be different if she'd reached out to you personally."

"You mean 'us'? Why did you single me out?"

"I meant us."

Hattie leaned back in her chair. "Naw, you did it twice. You're hiding somethin'."

Isaiah stared blankly.

"Boy, don't you lie to me. Whatchu hidin'?"

"All right. Don't get mad, but off and on over the years, I've been keeping in touch with Lisa."

Hattie gasped. "How long?"

"'Bout four, almost five, years," he whispered.

"What!" she shrieked.

Isaiah took a deep breath. He had planned to tell his mother, but didn't know when or how. "When you first told me about getting Christopher out of juvie, or what have you, I tried to find her. I thought she was still in Mississippi, but when he said Virginia, I looked there. It took me a little while, but I knew once you said juvie and he couldn't find his mama, I knew that was not LeeLee. Once I tracked her down, of course she confirmed it, but, yeah, we've been talking ever since."

Hattie wanted to beat the dog shit out of him, but she was tired. She hadn't slept much at all last night, and she worried about how her baby girl would react to her showing up unannounced after being absent for the last twenty-three years of her life. And now this? Isaiah had been keeping tabs on his sister without saying anything to her? So now she was the only neglectful, cold-hearted member of the family.

Hattie got up from the table and went to her room. She closed the door behind her. She was beyond livid. Hattie wanted to scream, but didn't want to up her pressure.

Clarence returned to the kitchen and looked at Isaiah. He shook his head and tsked. Isaiah rolled his eyes and got up to leave. Clarence then walked upstairs to check on his woman, but was met by a locked door. He shuffled back downstairs and watched the television on mute, in case he was beckoned.

* * *

Hattie fell asleep with the door locked, unintentionally keeping Clarence out of the bedroom and away from her. When she woke up around nine, she went downstairs, still a little upset, but immediately started laughing. Clarence was sprawled out on the couch, with one leg and arm hanging off, fast asleep in his polka dot underwear and undershirt. Her giggles woke him up.

"Whatchu laughing at, woman?" he grumbled.

"I'm sorry. I didn't mean to leave you out here in yo drawers." Hattie could barely get the sentence out before she started laughing uncontrollably. He joined in, then she really had tears rolling down her cheeks. Hattie went over to Clarence and kissed him on his forehead. "Thank you. I needed that."

Clarence slapped her across the rear and she hollered in delight.

Hattie didn't hear Christopher come in. "Ewe. Get a room."

"Get your own house," she snapped back. Christopher closed his mouth and started out of the room before Hattie stopped him. "We're going on a trip in two weeks."

Christopher perked up. "Awe shoot. Where y'all going?"

"We *all* are going to Virginia."

"Me too?" Christopher asked; Hattie nodded. "Awe man. For what? Why I gotta go?"

"To meet—your sister."

Christopher shot her an empty gaze. He'd forgotten about the bombshell his "mother" dropped on him a year and a half ago. Christopher had always looked up to Isaiah *like* a brother, but to find out that he truly was his older brother—half-brother—and the fact that he hadn't heard from his mother since made him feel even worse. He continued to call Hattie his "grandma" since he always found comfort in that, and Hattie didn't mind. "Is *he* gonna be around?"

Hattie didn't need a billboard to figure out who "he" was. "Probably."

Clarence cut in. "'Course he will. Why you think she's going?"

"You're going back to him?" Christopher's question was dripping with disgust.

"Hell no! We're going to see Ruth Anne. They're throwing a surprise party for her, and we've been invited."

"I'm not going." He turned around and walked away with his fists balled up. He responded to Hattie's calls to him by slamming his bedroom door shut.

She turned to Clarence, just as confused as ever. "Well, ain't that some shit."

* * *

"Hello." Isaiah was pleasantly surprised to hear from his mother so quickly. Last time they had a disagreement, she didn't talk to him for three weeks. She only called then because her dishwasher broke down.

"I need you to do me a favor," Hattie mumbled.

He let her lack of pleasantries slide this time. If he pissed her off again, he probably wouldn't hear from her until his sister's fiftieth birthday. "What's that?"

"I need you to talk to your brother."

It was a bitter pill to swallow for Isaiah, finding out at forty-three years old that he had a brother. But he genuinely liked Christopher. He was a goofball, but then Isaiah probably was too at that age. "About what?"

"I decided to go to the party. I want us all to go, but Christopher don't want to."

"I'm not surprised. How did you ask him?"

"Whatchu mean?"

"I mean what I asked." Silence. "Mama," he paused to collect his thoughts. "Sometimes you come off a lil rough around the edges."

"How so?"

"When you ask people stuff, it's not really asking. You make it sound like a requirement, like we don't have a choice. Know what I'm saying?"

"So? What's wrong with that? If I ask you something, obviously I want it done."

"I know that, Mama. But you gotta soften it up some. You can't just go to him and say, 'Pack your bags. You're coming with us, okay?' He just found out—"

"Over a year ago!"

Isaiah sighed. "He found out after twenty-one years on God's green earth that he indeed had a father, not to mention siblings, and accidentally met half his family. It takes a while to process. He's probably still pissed off. You don't get it 'cause you know exactly where you came from." It was quiet on the other end, but he continued anyway. "He needs some time to process. This is a delicate situation. You're asking him to go on vacation to meet a sister he didn't even know he had, and to see his daddy again, who he's not very fond of. Plus, his mama is God knows where."

"I'll go." A voice behind Hattie startled her. She turned around and came face to face with Christopher. She dropped the phone, crossed the kitchen, and hugged him.

Once they pulled apart, Hattie had tears forming in her eyes. "I know that this is a delicate situation for you to process, you know, meeting a sister you didn't even know about and seeing your daddy, but we'll be there as a family." She squeezed his arm affectionately, as she heard a loud dial tone. Hattie ran over to the phone and called Isaiah back. "I'm sorry, baby. I forgot you was on the phone."

"What happened? Besides you repeating everything I said."

"We all set. Find us some tickets for the Friday after next. Clarence will meet us there."

"Ah shit, Mama! Whatchu bringing the country bumpkin for?"

*   *   *

Isaiah checked the family into their room at the Forty Doves Suites. Hattie and Clarence were in one room and the boys were sharing another. Christopher was itching to see what kind of amenities the hotel offered, so he ventured off by himself.

Christopher looked in every nook and cranny in his room, then headed back down to the lobby. He followed the signs to the indoor pool and fitness room. Christopher debated on getting a drink, since he was finally of age, but decided not to just yet. He wanted to just peek instead. Christopher stepped into the lounge and was immediately greeted by a hostess. He told her that he wasn't staying and turned to leave, but bumped into a face he vaguely recognized.

"Christopher, right?"

"Yeah. Benjamin, right?"

"Yes—your father."

"I'd like to go on Maury, first." Christopher tried to push past Benjamin but was stopped mid-stride.

"Hey mane, I'm just as angry as you are. I would've taken care of you if I had known you existed, but—"

"You knew about Isaiah and you didn't do nothin' for him," Christopher shot back.

Benjamin stopped. His son had a valid point, but that didn't stop the sting. "You right. I was a terrible father to Isaiah, but it's better late than never. I'm trying to make up for it."

"How, *Dad*?" Isaiah stepped up to the fellas and stood next to his brother. Christopher turned to him, grateful for the ally and surprised because he hadn't heard anyone coming up behind him. "You were gone for a while, so I was making sure you didn't get snatched up." He patted Christopher's shoulder. Turning back to Benjamin, "So what's this about making it up to me?"

"At the court, remember I tried to reach out to you—both of you. But the only person who called me was your mother. She's here, right?"

"Don't worry about Mama. She doesn't need you either." Isaiah stated matter-of-factly. "And she doesn't need you calling her all the time. I thought you were getting married?"

"Juanita and I went our separate ways. She can't be trusted."

"Then y'all were perfect for each other."

Benjamin huffed. "Look, I didn't come here to argue. I want—no, I need to make peace with y'all. It makes no sense not to get along with my only boys. So, how can I make it up to you? I'll do whatever."

The boys looked at each other, and Christopher decided to take the bait. "You can start by buying us a drink."

Benjamin smiled. "My pleasure." He slapped Christopher on the back and was met with a nasty grimace. The three men took a seat at the bar. Isaiah wished Christopher hadn't given in so easily, but was happy to put his wallet away.

*   *   *

Clarence trailed Benjamin's car to Lisa's condo complex's clubhouse, apart from the townhouses. Clarence, salty due to the mere presence of Benjamin, tailgated him the whole ride. Benjamin wanted to slam on the brakes but was afraid of getting into an accident in his rental. Clarence apparently didn't care either way. The family filed out of their cars and stood in the parking lot. Hattie froze with fear.

"Mae, come on now. You've made it this far," Benjamin coaxed her.

Not to be outdone, "Yeah, baby," said Clarence, and kissed her on the cheek. "We'll be right by your side." Benjamin and Isaiah rolled their eyes.

"Just a lil nervous, that's all. What if she gets mad when she sees me and I ruin the whole party? What if—"

"You'll be just fine, Mama. I promise. I'm sure she misses you as much as you miss her. Come on." Isaiah grabbed her hand, tucked it under his arm, and guided her to the clubhouse. Christopher ran over to Hattie's other side and put his arm around her. Hattie teared up at the love and support from her boys.

The five of them walked into the party in a huddle, with Benjamin leading the pack. They each signed the guest book as instructed. Benjamin appeared to be the man; he introduced the family to almost everyone in the room. When they came to a gorgeous cocoa-colored female and a tall, trim male, Benjamin pulled them to each side of him by their shoulders.

"I'd like to give these two a special introduction." He turned to the two people and spoke to them first. "Now, remember I told y'all I have some folks I wanted you to meet?" The two nodded. Hattie sniffed, trying to hold back both tears and snot. "First, I want you all to say hello to your grandmother. Hattie Mae, this is Gerri and Brandon."

The two stuck out their hands to introduce themselves, but Hattie grabbed them both for a suffocating hug. A handshake was unacceptable—not for their first meeting or anytime afterward. They were flesh and blood, for God's sake. The two hugged back and were even receptive to their grandmother's cheek kisses. No words were exchanged yet; Hattie couldn't find them, except to repeatedly thank Jesus.

Once Hattie finally let her grandchildren go, Benjamin went on to introduce Christopher and Isaiah. The children happily embraced

Isaiah tightly, since they had spoken numerous times before. "Good to see y'all again," Isaiah gushed. He wrapped his arms around their shoulders like the proud uncle that he was.

Hattie grabbed Gerri's hand and stared at her. "My God. You look *just* like Ruth Anne." Before Gerri could respond, the lights turned off. Suddenly, the room filled with murmurs of "Shh" and "Hide," but the family froze, uncertain of where to go.

A woman's voice appeared, clearly annoyed as she spoke on the phone. "I don't know why Simon told me to come here. He ain't even here. Have you—"

"*Surprise!*" the crowd shouted when someone turned the lights back on. Lisa dropped the phone and put her hands up to her face. The man who hit the lights went over and kissed her.

"Happy birthday, babes," he grinned, and Lisa playfully hit him in the chest.

"You just shaved five years off of my life!" The group laughed and clapped, then broke into Stevie Wonder's version of "Happy Birthday." She hugged the man but released early from the embrace. Lisa's smile vanished. The celebratory song was cut short as she slowly crossed to the center of the room. "Mama?"

Hattie tried to blink away the tears, but to no avail. She held out her arms, but was left hanging. Instead, she received a slap to the face. The crowd gasped. The slap stung, both inside and out. Surprise and shame had Hattie in a chokehold.

Simon tried to hold his wife back, but she pushed him away. Lisa stood inches away from her mother. Clarence took a step closer to his woman.

"I know you're angry, and you have every right to be," Hattie's voice shook.

"You damn right, but that's not even the half of it. I can't believe that you have the audacity to show your face here. How dare you!"

Hattie continued—scared but determined. "I thought about you every day. Don't think that I haven't. I have loved you every single day. And I have missed you. It wasn't right for me to let you go twenty years ago."

"Twenty-three," Lisa corrected through her tears.

"Yes, twenty-three." Hattie paused to collect her thoughts. "And you didn't 'let me go,' you kicked me out! There's a big difference. You kicked out your own child. Your baby girl. How do you even sleep at night?"

"NyQuil." The two broke out into loud laughter and hugged each other tight. "I'm so sorry, baby," Hattie chanted.

Simon, who was holding his breath, finally exhaled, but was totally confused by Lisa's actions. Despite knowing that his wife had harbored anger toward her mother for years, he also knew deep down that she longed for her. The void was now filled. Simon was almost brought to tears himself at the bizarre but touching reconciliation. *Strange Americans*, he shook his head.

Lisa broke from her mother and grabbed her hand. "I see you've already met my babies." She wiped tears off her face and Gerri's, then turned to Simon. "So, I'd like you to meet my wonderful and deceitful husband, Simon."

"Deceitful? Why *deceitful*," his Jamaican accent was part of the reason Lisa fell in love with him.

"'Candlelight dinner' my foot!" The family laughed.

"Okay, I see where you're coming from." He shook and kissed the back of Hattie's hand. Clarence was now shoulder-to-shoulder with Hattie and kept a watchful eye on the foreigner. "It's very nice to meet you, Ms. Atkins. I'm so glad you came. Just want you to know that you have blessed me with such a wonderful wife and I truly thank you for that. Fada too." He turned to Benjamin and smiled. Hattie and her crew looked totally confused. "That's *father* where I come from."

"How did you find them?" Lisa asked her husband. She grabbed Isaiah's hand and placed her head on his shoulder.

"Thank your fada. He did all the legwork. I only made a *strong* suggestion that they join us. I just wanted to give you a gift that I haven't given you before, sweetness." He winked at his wife.

Benjamin spoke up. "Baby Doll, I want to introduce you to someone else you should know." He grabbed Christopher by the arm and pulled him close to him. Christopher accepted his father putting his hands on him; Hattie squinted. *Now all of a sudden everybody's Team Wild Cat? Must've missed that memo.* "This is Christopher. He's your brother, well, half-brother. I know I mentioned him before but couldn't wait for you guys to meet in person," Benjamin explained. Lisa hugged Christopher and he reciprocated with a smile.

"I'm so overwhelmed with joy and have so many questions. But for now, let's party! Come on guys." Still holding onto Hattie, she grabbed Isaiah's hand to lead them into the crowd. "I wanna introduce you to—"

"Already done. I took them around to meet everyone." Clarence cleared his throat. "Oh yeah," Benjamin rolled his eyes. "This is your mama's friend, Clarence."

"Gentleman caller," he stuck out his hand and shook hers. "Pleased to make your acquaintance." He then kissed her hand and all of the men looked ready to pounce. Clarence took a step back.

Lisa gave her father a hug and a quick kiss, then latched onto Hattie again. "Mama, I'm so happy you came. Having my whole family together after all these years is the best gift anyone could've given me. How long are you here for?"

"Till Sunday."

"That's not long enough." Lisa pouted. Hattie thought, *Same ole Ruth Anne. Loved to pout.* "Before you go, can you at least come over tomorrow for church and brunch?"

"We're here until five. Sounds better than the stale muffins and toast at the hotel!" The two women hugged again and the men smiled.

This was the happiest Benjamin had ever seen Lisa and Hattie. He was overjoyed that their feud had finally come to an end, but heartsick that this time tomorrow, he would be home alone again. *If there was only some way I can get the family together again—permanently.*

Silver Bells

Let us therefore make every effort to do what leads to peace and to mutual edification. (Romans 14:19)

"You're doing what, now?" Hattie screeched.

Isaiah didn't know whether she was happy or upset. Either way, her voice pierced his eardrums and he moved the phone away as he contemplated his next move. He decided to tread lightly. "I said I'm getting married." Silence. "Mama?"

"I heard you," she snapped.

"Oh, 'cause I didn't—"

"Just didn't know what to say."

"Oh, okay. And?"

"And the answer is no," she stated matter-of-factly.

"I didn't ask for *your* hand in marriage," he laughed. Isaiah just *knew* she was joking. "How can you give an answer? I just wanted to know what you thought about it."

"How the hell are you gonna get married and I didn't even know you were dating? Is it that Storm heffa?"

"Raine," he rolled his eyes. They'd been through this before. And obviously, since she guessed in the general vicinity of her name, she knew a little more than she was letting on. "Yes, she accepted my proposal this past weekend."

"And you waited three whole days to tell me? The hell is wrong witchu?"

"Mama—"

"Not to mention the fact that I haven't even met her yet. Whatchu hidin' her for? What's wrong with her? Besides that raggedy-ass name."

"Mama—"

"She ugly?"

Isaiah huffed. "See, this is why you haven't met her! You're so—"

"You've only been with her for five minutes."

He cut her off. "Try five years." He heard his mother gasp. "She's a beautiful Black woman who I can't wait to make my queen. She's intelligent, sweet, down to earth, no kids. You would actually like her if you could just look past her name for half a second."

"That still doesn't explain why you cut me outta your personal life."

"Mama, I didn't cut you out. Stop being so dramatic. You've never liked anybody I've dated. They were always too ugly, too loud, too skinny, too cross-eyed—*something*! So I decided not to bring anyone around anymore."

"But I—"

"Plus, this one is special. I had to make sure she was right and that she met your standards before I brought her home."

"Humph!" More silence. "So *am I* going to meet her before you elope?" Hattie snapped.

"Who said anything about eloping? We're gonna exchange vows right at the house."

"Whose house?"

*   *   *

Hattie sat in her favorite spot, pouting. She rocked in her chair like it had never been rocked before. She'd had her baby boy to herself for over forty years. *Why couldn't he wait another thirty years until he buried me to get married?* It's not that she didn't want to see Isaiah happy and in love; it was much deeper than that. But Hattie couldn't quite put her finger on it.

The phone rang beside her. Thinking it was Isaiah calling to tell her that the whole thing was a joke, she answered on the first ring.

"You changed your mind!"

"Uh, Hattie," the confused caller questioned.

"Bea?"

"Yeah?"

"Ah shit! Thought you were Isaiah."

"Oh, I was gonna ask you what I missed." Bea laughed; Hattie didn't. Hattie always enjoyed preaching the Word and gossiping with her bestie, but now wasn't the time. Bea didn't catch on. "I wanted to see what time you wanted to go over to Flo's tonight."

Hattie had forgotten all about it. She and a few of her church bosom buddies threw luncheons for new members as a welcome. They did it to be nice, but mostly to disguise their nosiness when they went over to the unsuspecting members' houses. They really wanted to see who they could recruit into their clique.

"I can't make it."

"Why not? You always go," Bea whined.

"I'm not feeling too good. Let me know how it goes."

"What's wrong, Hattie? Need me to bring you some soup? Or go over some verses? Lemme get my Bible out right quick."

"No, Bea. I'll be alright." After some unrelenting pleas from her friend, Hattie finally told her about Isaiah. She couldn't understand why his good news would get her "panties in a bunch," as she called it. Trying to explain got on Hattie's nerves and caused her to hang up on her friend. She mumbled obscenities to no one in particular, and stayed stationary in her spot for the better part of the day, ignoring her nightly call from Clarence and her Wednesday night TV lineup. Upset for being so upset, she finally made her way upstairs to wash up and hit the sack.

*   *   *

Hattie was in such a funk for the next few days that she didn't fully realize that Christopher was in and out of the house that weekend. Now that he'd found a girlfriend, he was hardly ever at home. She fussed every time he spent the night away from home, *knowing* that he was out sinning. And he fussed every time he would come home during dinnertime to find no dinner.

Hattie's cooking had slowed down tremendously since she didn't have as much foot traffic from her weekly visits from Isaiah and Christopher staying there part-time. Could it be that she was experiencing empty nest syndrome? Could that have stirred up her bitterness?

"Hey, grandma. I made you something." She wondered when Christopher would ever feel comfortable calling her Mama, but didn't push it.

Hattie cautiously stepped into the kitchen. Christopher had never cooked for her without her asking him to. She wondered what she had done to deserve this. *Oh Lord, am I on my way out?* "Whatchu got for me?"

He lifted the lid of the biggest pot. "I made some chili." He peeled back a corner of a pan covered in foil. "Cornbread. And for dessert—banana pudding."

She side-eyed him. "When did you make all this? I can't be that deaf. Usually you have some rap crap blasting down here, and I certainly didn't hear you drop any pots on the floor like you usually do."

"Well, I brought the banana pudding from Lesha's house and—"

"Okay, I won't be eating that."

"Why not?"

"Her hands dirty."

"What are you talking about? You weren't there. And it's good, like yours."

"Don't compare mine to hers. I make masterpieces, and she makes"—Hattie peeked at the big bowl of pudding—"play dough."

Christopher groaned and shook his head. Instead of arguing, he decided to change the subject to get her in good spirits. "So did Isaiah tell you the good news?"

Hattie scooped three big spoonfuls of chili into a bowl and plopped a slice of cornbread on top. "What good news?"

"He's getting married! That's dope, ain't it?"

"Big whoop." She licked the spoon and sat down at the table. Famished, she'd forgotten that she hadn't eaten since yesterday afternoon, so she didn't waste any time. To Christopher, it sounded like pigs slopping. He guessed it was safe to assume that she liked his rendition of one of her favorite meals.

"'Big whoop'? You're not happy for him?"

"I don't want to talk about it."

He took a deep breath and blurted out, "You don't like to see no one happy!" Hattie dropped her spoon and turned to face her accuser.

Shit. My mouth gets me in trouble every time. That's the Juanita coming out of me, Christopher cursed himself.

"Boy, don't you *ever* badmouth me, you hear?" She rose out of her seat and headed toward him. Christopher slightly cowered, but she grabbed the salt over his shoulder. He relaxed. *WAP!* She swung anyway and landed an open hand on the back of his head. The slap both shocked and stung Christopher. Tears welled up in his eyes. He had never been slapped before, especially by a heavy-handed heavyweight. Sure, she had swung her Bible at him a few times over the years, but an open-handed slap to the head? No ma'am. Hattie looked away and continued. "I'm so sick and tired of your smart mouth. Have some respect for your damn elders."

"I'm not Isaiah."

Confused, "I know that. Isaiah knows better than to talk to me any kind of way. You the crazy one."

"No, I mean—never mind." He stopped himself before he dug any deeper. Instead, he mumbled, "I would never hit my little boy like that."

Before Hattie could sit, she turned back to Christopher. "What lil boy?"

Stuttering, "I mean, if I were to have one." *This is not how I wanted it to come out.*

"Back it up, boy. You hiding somethin', now out with it." She walked slowly over to Christopher, pointing a spoon in his face.

He realized that he was now cornered—literally and figuratively. Christopher took a deep breath and spilled the beans. "Lesha's pregnant. We're having a lil boy."

The words couldn't come out just yet, but if looks could kill, Christopher would be fifty feet deep. He placed a cautious hand on her shoulder to reason with her, but that only set her off. "Are you serious"—she wanted to snatch Christopher up, but stopped herself. "Hold up! If you already know what you're having, that means that you've known for quite some time, haven't you?" She didn't really want a response. He dropped his head. "Sonuva bitch!" Hattie collapsed back down in her seat. With her nostrils flaring, she glared straight ahead while placing her fiery face in her open palm.

Christopher knew that silence was key. He was well aware of the story of how she'd reacted to Lisa, or LeeLee as Isaiah called her, once she shared her news, and he didn't want history to repeat itself. He thought it wouldn't be as bad since he was older than Lisa was when she ended up pregnant. Christopher wanted to be open and honest with the woman who had been kind enough to care for him over the past five years, but he was also truly terrified of her, and she knew it. In fact, he felt that she fed off of others' fear like a crazed pit bull. Plus, his head still stung.

On the other hand, Christopher knew deep down that Hattie cared more than she put on. He wished that she would show that side more when he really needed her to have his back. This was definitely one of those times, especially because of how scared he and Lesha were. They had been together for two years and genuinely loved each other, but the thought of bringing a baby into the world before he could get a better job or own his own place was alarming.

"I was thinking about popping the question, you know, to make an honest woman out of her"—Hattie snickered; he ignored her and continued—"before my baby comes, but I gotta move out first. That's really what I've been saving for."

"You think you've made enough for rent, gas, lights, school, you, a wife, *and* a baby?" She finally looked at him. "Nothing can prepare you for the type of debt you're about to be in. And what happened to school? Just threw yo life away. Thought I did better this time." Christopher looked like he'd peed himself, so she decided to take another approach. She backed off.

Hattie was scared too, but a different kind. She knew what it was like to raise children with two parents in the home *and* with only one. She knew that love didn't always last forever. And she knew how much she hated to see the first and the fifteenth come around. Hattie didn't have others to lean on financially after Benjamin left, and she couldn't imagine what Lisa went through when she disowned her at seventeen. Hattie wanted Christopher to realize that raising children was no picnic, but she also didn't want him and Lesha to go at it alone like she'd made her own daughter do.

She decided to do something she should've done years ago with Lisa. She hobbled over to Christopher. He flinched, but then softened like butter as Hattie hugged him. He drenched her shoulder with tears. With emotion filling her to the brim, she let loose as well—for Lisa, for Christopher, for Isaiah, for herself.

*   *   *

Christopher and Hattie continued talking through dinner and for an hour afterward. They discussed everything from their favorite movies, to future plans, to their darkest fears and regrets. Naturally, Hattie's number one regret was her scandalous mistake in kicking Lisa out, but what she'd discovered since was that her ultimate fear was being alone.

She admitted that she never forgave herself for what she'd done to Lisa, but if she had it her way, Isaiah would never have left the house either. Hattie hated the fact that he moved out within the same week as the Lisa incident; she described it as a piece of her dying inside. It was easily the worst period of her life.

Christopher slept better that night than he had since Lesha told him she was pregnant. Finally rid of the burden of his secret, he felt not only relieved but also closer to Hattie than ever before. Christopher finally understood where Hattie was coming from. All she really wanted was for her family to be close and for her to be needed. He let her know that he wasn't going anywhere just yet and would use his savings to take care of his responsibilities. Hattie liked the new "grown man" Christopher, and he appreciated the "wise old woman" as his brother often called her.

Hattie looked more rested the next morning—unburdening your soul and having a good cry can go a long way. It felt good to get everything off her chest. Her guilt about Lisa and feeling left out of Isaiah's life had been a lot to carry on her shoulders for so long. Sure, she talked to Bea, but they only scraped the surface most times. Nothing was better than talking freely to family. Now that Hattie and Lisa were talking again, Isaiah's engagement had really thrown her for a loop, but he was grown and had his mind made up, so there was nothing left to do but to support him. After living seventy-one years, she had to learn the hard way how important support was in a loving relationship. Hattie felt truly blessed with the family she had.

Christopher woke up to Hattie's infamous chocolate chip pancakes, grits, bacon, eggs, sausage, hash browns, and biscuits. He smiled as the wonderful scents beckoned him. He swung his legs over his bed and shuffled into the kitchen. A wide grin spread across his face once he saw a man's head buried in a plate.

"About time you got your lazy butt up, boy," Isaiah joked between chews. The two men shook hands. "We're behind you five hundred percent." He wiped his mouth. "Can't wait to be an uncle again. Me and Raine can babysit anytime." Isaiah stood to hug his brother.

Hattie put the works on a plate across from Isaiah and motioned for Christopher to sit. She then fixed her own plate and joined the conversation about what to name her great grandson, or whatever she would be to him. Her vote was for Abraham, but that was quickly vetoed by the men. Hattie gave up and listened to her boys go back and forth. She smiled, wishing that her daughter was there to complete the picture.

She had been on the fence about Clarence. Some days she liked him and other days he got on her nerves. Maybe it was the stress of carrying on a long-distance relationship. Either way, she wasn't sure what to do with his suggestion about making the move to Michigan to be closer to her, cause she damn sure wasn't going down there. For now, she enjoyed her space, and her focus was on rebuilding her family.

* * *

"I am so nervous," Raine confided in her fiancé.

"Don't be, babe. Just remember what I told you," Isaiah reassured her as they walked to Hattie's door. He affectionately caressed her cheek and kissed it. Before he could put the key in, the door swung open.

"Sup, bruh," Christopher shook hands and hugged his brother. "Hey new sis, or shall I say, soon-to-be sis." Isaiah introduced the two and stepped into the house. Once Christopher shut the door,

Hattie stood in the middle of the floor, just looking. She had been waiting for this moment for some time now. Both happiness and dread consumed her. She hadn't initially been impressed with Raine, but her smile could soften anyone, even Hattie.

"So this is the woman who's gonna take my baby away." Hattie didn't mean to say that out loud, but since her weak secret came to light, *we'll see how this plays out*, she thought.

"Grandma, behave yourself," Christopher whispered over his shoulder to her.

"It's so nice to meet you, Ms. Atkins. I promise not to take him from you. I'm simply adding a little sunshine to his life."

"With rain?"

"With Raine," she smiled.

"Come in and have a seat," Christopher stated, and led the group to the family room. He played the perfect host and took Raine's coat to hang up; Isaiah draped his on the arm of the sofa. The family sat down to polite conversation, until Hattie asked where they were going to live. Isaiah started to answer, but Raine took the lead.

"I've always said that I'd never pick up and move for a man, but that was before I met the right one. Isaiah means the world to me and I know you feel the same—well, in a different way—and I'd like to keep him happy. So after our honeymoon, I will officially move into his house, so that we can be close to home. If that's alright with you, of course."

"Fine by me." Hattie fought back a smile. "Let me make you some tea, honey." She left the room and all eyes fell on Isaiah.

"What did I tell you?" He smiled and kissed the back of Raine's hand. "I would never steer you wrong. Can't wait till tomorrow to make you my wife." The couple hugged. Christopher suddenly missed Lesha.

*   *   *

The next day, Christmas Eve, was the biggest day of Isaiah's life, and he had been looking forward to it since he turned thirty. He couldn't wait to share his life with his soulmate. All he wanted was for everything to go smoothly and on time.

"Come on, Mama." Isaiah knocked loudly on Christopher's door. Since it was his bright idea to get married at his mother's house, Raine and her bridal party were getting ready upstairs, while Hattie was forced to use the downstairs bathroom and Christopher's room. Christopher and Lesha were obligated to use the laundry room to change, after being harassed by Hattie not to fool around in there.

Hattie was in one of her moods. She fussed about strange people coming in and out of her house. She fussed about being put out of her own bedroom. She fussed about Isaiah getting hitched on a holiday.

"Whoever heard of such. Any other Christmas Eve, I would be sitting my ass in church and cooking for my family." Hattie swung the door open—still fussing.

"Yeah, cussing and all, huh?"

"Get out of my way, boy." She paused to take a closer look at her handsome son in his black tux and her eyes glistened. "My word."

"Yeah, um, hello. This is supposed to be a big deal for me, remember?" He rolled his eyes. "You act like I do this every Christmas Eve. This is a one-shot deal."

"Would you two knock it off?" Lisa rounded the corner and swatted at her big brother. "Don't you have somewhere to be? They're about to start the music." Isaiah nervously bit his lip and took off. "And you, let's find our seats. Shall we?" She hooked her mother's arm into hers and they walked toward the sliding door into the family room.

Hattie couldn't imagine a winter wedding happening outside, but was immensely impressed once she approached the door. Since neither Isaiah nor Raine had invited a lot of guests, there was plenty of room to host them in the breathtaking tent. Thankfully, Michigan was having a mild winter, so snow didn't have to be shoveled before the tent was set up. From the lit candles, shimmery pillars, and a flower-flooded gazebo, the space couldn't look more amazing, and Hattie couldn't be happier for her son.

Isaiah's childhood friend Alan began playing on his keyboard once he saw Hattie and Lisa in the doorway. The guests quieted down and took their seats. Lisa had suggested that she walk down the aisle with Hattie, since Clarence and Benjamin were fighting over the task. Lisa escorted her mother to the front row, and they took their seats in front of Simon, Sis Bea, and Clarence. Benjamin scooted down to the end, under Clarence's watchful eyes. Christopher and Brandon quickly took their seats after ushering everyone in.

Isaiah walked in and met Pastor Stanley up front. Tears trickled down Hattie's chubby cheeks; Lisa took her hand. Raine's best friend, Pam, and Isaiah's best friend, Jay, walked in after Raine's parents, whom Hattie had the pleasure of meeting briefly before the ceremony. The couple had decided to keep things simple: twenty guests, including a best man and a matron of honor, and no ring bearer, bridesmaids, or groomsmen. Colors didn't matter to the couple, so the wedding party was instructed to dress any way they pleased. Lisa's daughter, Gerri, served as a seasoned flower girl. The role tickled her, as she thoroughly enjoyed having all eyes on her as if she were the one getting married.

Once the music changed to Intro's version of "Ribbon in the Sky," the crowd rose to their feet. The doors slid open and in walked Raine in a lavender satin gown with a bateau neckline and gem-encrusted waistband. Hattie was shocked and in awe. The dress was gorgeous, but she wondered why she didn't wear white like every other bride. *People always got to be difficult,* Hattie shook her head and Lisa pinched her. Shook by the role reversal, Hattie straightened up in her seat and fixed her face.

"You all may be seated," Pastor Stanley spoke. "Let us begin with a prayer. Everyone please bow your heads." Once the pastor was finished, Lisa took his place at the altar.

"Thank you all for sharing your Christmas Eve with my family on this glorious day. It's a great honor to stand before you and read this poem I wrote for my brother and his queen. It's a poem about laughter, partnership, friendship, sacrifice, forgiveness, and most of all, love."

*   *   *

Once Pastor Stanley pronounced Isaiah and Raine as husband and wife, Hattie really boo-hooed. The guests followed the couple inside the house. Isaiah and Raine were escorted upstairs so their photo session wouldn't be interrupted, and the rest of the crowd was ushered into the basement for the reception. When the coast was clear, the newlyweds rejoined the family for additional pictures.

"Well, I did it, Mama." Isaiah hugged his mother and kissed her on the cheek.

"Yeah, yeah, yeah."

"I saw you crying up a storm. What's wrong with you? You happy or something?" he teased.

Hattie dabbed her eyes, embarrassed. "Leave me alone, boy. It's these allergies." His second kiss was met with a playful push.

Niecy, the church's photographer, placed the family and wedding party in all sorts of combinations during their photo session. The only one who wasn't included was Clarence. He sat quietly off to the side, but not far. The only reason Benjamin was in two pictures (and invited) was because Hattie insisted, which made Clarence's blood boil. *She didn't fight for me to be in any pictures and I've been around Isaiah longer than his own daddy,* Clarence thought angrily.

Once Niecy finished, Lisa's kids hustled down into the basement to join the rest of the party. Clarence grabbed Hattie's arm and pulled her to the side. Conveniently, in front of her children and Benjamin, Clarence wobbled down to one knee and clasped her hand. The family gasped.

"Hattie, would you—"

"Would you get up, you ole fool!"

Upset, he struggled to pick himself up and confronted her. "Do you know what you just did?"

"Yes, and this is not the time for that."

"Well, when?"

"I don't know. But it's tacky to do this at someone else's wedding. We'll steal their thunder."

"Naw, Mama. Go head, Clarence," Isaiah prodded. He wanted to know where this was going, and no time was better than the present.

Hattie glared at her son. She then looked over at Benjamin, who was hanging on everybody's word.

"See, I knew it." Clarence pointed at Hattie.

"Knew what?"

"I knew there was something going on. Whatchu looking at him for?"

"At who?"

"Don't play with me, woman. That's why you won't let me move here. You still got feelings for ole Casper."

"Casper?" Benjamin questioned.

"You *left* your family, so in my book, you've *earned* that name," Clarence declared. Isaiah laughed. Benjamin took a step toward him, but Lisa grabbed his arm. "But don't think that I'ma just roll over. This here is *my* woman." He turned back to Hattie. "You might not want to marry me today, but you betta believe I will marry you. Mark my words." He headed toward the house. "Let's go in here and get somethin' to eat. I'm starved."

The family looked at this unhinged man. For Clarence to have the gall to call out Benjamin and Hattie and then walk away to fix his plate was wild. As much as Hattie was disgusted, she was also turned on by his sudden take-charge attitude and tried to fight back a smile. She would thank him privately later.

*   *   *

The following March, Hattie attended Lesha's baby shower. She sat uncomfortably with a bunch of "teeny boppers," as she called the young crowd of the couple's friends. Hattie was the oldest one there, and that was including Lesha's grandmother. The newlyweds were out of town and Lisa was at a work conference, so she was left to embrace the silly shit, as she called it, by herself. Hattie hated these showers, wedding and baby alike, and preferred to be at church with her own friends.

Lesha's mother sliced up some cake, and they finally reached the gift-opening part. So far, they'd received a diaper cake, some clothes, and a few bibs and booties. Next was Hattie's gift.

"Ooh, this one's small. What could this be?" Lesha teased. Christopher took a seat next to his girlfriend, anxious to see what was in the box she was shaking. Lesha ripped off the wrapping paper and gasped. *CLICK!* Her mother took a picture of the gift before realizing what it was.

Christopher looked at Hattie. "A box of condoms. Really?"

"You said, 'something you needed.'"

You Never Know

Every good and perfect gift is from above, coming down from the Father of the heavenly lights, who does not change like shifting shadows.
(James 1:17)

"You would make me the happiest man on earth if you were to marry me. Hattie, you know I love you more than water." The couple sat on a park bench well after sunset.

"Oh, stop that," Hattie giggled and shyly turned her head to blush.

The man's familiar voice sashayed in her ear. "I just can't be without you any longer. Don't hold us back from a chance at pure happiness. Just marry me." He pushed an opened velvet ring box toward her. The diamond twinkled in her eyes. She clasped her hands over her round cheeks. *This is happening, isn't it?* "Believe it, baby." He could read her thoughts, too? Damn!

She looked up at the handsome man and jumped out of her seat. "Wild Cat?"

"Yeah, who else did you think it could be?"

"Oh, shit!" Hattie violently sat up in her bed, drenched in sweat. She looked all around the room and saw no signs of Benjamin or Clarence. "What the hell is going on?" she grumbled.

Hattie attempted to swing her legs out of bed, but was met with a sharp pain in her chest. "Ouch!" Fully awake now, she pressed her chest to calm the pain, but made it worse. Through the pain, she twisted her body to get out of bed and opened her bedroom door. Hattie called out to Christopher but received no answer. She grabbed the cordless phone and dialed 911. Before she could speak, she lost her footing and took a hard tumble down the stairs.

What seemed like a minute later was actually twenty. The 911 operator sent a rescue team to Hattie's when they didn't receive a response over the phone and heard some enormous thumps. Hattie opened her bewildered eyes to a bunch of people tugging on her and a breathing mask on her face. She scanned the room but was afraid to move too much. Hattie felt disoriented and sick to her stomach. She closed her eyes again when she felt the stretcher taking her on a ride.

*   *   *

The next time Hattie opened her eyes, she was in the hospital. Isaiah sat next to her on her bed, staring at her. Christopher, Raine, Lesha, and Christopher's three-month-old son, CJ, were gathered around the room and perked up once they saw Hattie awake. Isaiah saw her attempting to speak, but stopped her. He knew she was about to fuss … about anything.

"Hey, Mama. You're in the hospital," he whispered. Her brows scrunched up. "You had a mild heart attack, fell down the stairs, and bumped your head." Hattie's eyes widened. "It's okay, Mama. You're okay. You'll have to take it easy, okay?" Her face stayed scrunched. "You'll feel some soreness 'cause they did a procedure on you, but everything's okay now."

Christopher attempted to chime in but was scared to come any closer. He hated hospitals, and the tubes and wires everywhere made him nervous. "And you even got a fancy head wrap from when you bumped your head." Hattie rolled her eyes. *At least she's back to normal.*

The family tried to normalize the situation as much as they could, as if they were in Hattie's family room playing catch-up. They talked politics, talked about their jobs and other happenings. An hour and a half passed, and they said their farewells for now. Hattie was rather glum about seeing her family leave, but she was exhausted. She fell asleep before the door closed.

*   *   *

A few days later, Hattie was being wheeled out of the hospital to Isaiah's truck. She had to stay a little longer so they could monitor her head injury, and of course her heart. She fussed and cussed all throughout the hospital, insisting that she knew how to walk. That was hardly the only thing she complained about during her stay. Hattie dropped nine pounds after refusing to eat the food the hospital supplied. She likened the pillows and sheets to paper. And anytime a nurse stopped by to take her vitals or wake her up to dispense medicine, Hattie pitched one. The hospital staff threw a party when she was discharged, including Jello shots that they claimed didn't contain liquor. It had been a long five days for all!

"Surprise!" her family quietly yelled. The whole gang was at the house, including Lisa and Benjamin. Isaiah had increased contact with Lisa after her birthday party, and she passed the message onto Benjamin. Benjamin would have taken a flight out that night if Lisa didn't ask him to wait for her so they could travel together. Isaiah planned to keep a close eye on his father. He seemed too up in his mama's business; it felt like he was trying to inch his way back in. Hattie often brushed it off, but always with a smirk. Low-key, Isaiah thought she liked the attention. In this case, he didn't trust either of them.

Even though Isaiah couldn't stand Clarence, he figured he had to call him too. Hattie wouldn't let him hear the end of it if he didn't. When Clarence arrived at the house, he gave Isaiah an enormous bear hug that left a foul taste in his mouth. Clarence looked like he'd aged a few years since Isaiah saw him six months ago, but Isaiah guessed that was the price you paid for dating Hattie Mae Atkins.

One by one, family members hugged Hattie long and gently when she walked in the door. She smiled and held onto each one for dear life. When they were released, she stared at each person as if she were etching their faces into her memory again. Benjamin and Clarence both attempted to go last. Their "friendly" competition got on everyone's nerves, including Hattie's. At first, she enjoyed the attention, but it quickly got old. She knew exactly what was going on.

"Wild Cat," Hattie held out her hand to him. Clarence wasn't too keen on her using his little nickname and he damn near snapped his neck trying to see where Benjamin would put her hand. Once Benjamin connected with Hattie, Clarence narrowed his eyes and moved closer. Benjamin kissed Hattie's cheek, and they warmly embraced. He whispered something that only the two of them heard.

Isaiah and Christopher stood close, staring as if they were watching a movie. Christopher elbowed Isaiah and tsked. Isaiah shook his head. *My money's on Pops—I mean, Benjamin.*

Hattie let go of Benjamin to hug Clarence. "Hey, Woman!" Benjamin stepped back just as Clarence bumped past him. Isaiah grabbed Benjamin's shoulders and twisted him around to walk away. Choosing to be oblivious, Hattie and Clarence hugged and kissed, but not as long as she and Benjamin. She squirmed out of his arms after two Mississippis, and Clarence wasn't the only one who noticed. Benjamin smirked.

"This was all such a big surprise. If I had known everybody was gonna be here, I would've—"

Isaiah cut in. "Don't say it, Mama."

"I won't. I'll just say that I would've had some food in the refrigerator, that's all." The family laughed. "I just want to thank y'all for coming and for being here for me. I really 'preciate you all. Do y'all have a moment to sit down? You know, chill out a bit?"

"'Chill out'? What was you watching in the hospital, BET?" Christopher cracked, and everyone laughed. Hattie hugged and kissed him, which was something she did only occasionally, but he loved it when it happened. The family gathered into the family room and sat around Hattie to laugh, cry, and talk some more.

*   *   *

Two hours later, the house cleared out except for Clarence, Isaiah, and Benjamin. Raine dropped Lisa off at the hotel to get some sleep. Hattie's suitors were revving up for round two on who would take Isaiah home until he mentioned spending the night.

"Oh," Benjamin's eyes roamed the floor. "You beat me to the punch."

"You already got a room. Whatchu need to stay here with my lady for?" questioned Clarence with his broad chest stuck out like a bird.

"How you know what I got?" The men stood, although Clarence could easily rest his head on Benjamin's shoulder.

"Oh please. None of y'all need to stay the night, but I'm fine with Isaiah being here. At least I won't have to deal with this mess the rest of the night." Hattie struggled to get out of her chair, shooing away everyone who tried to help. She shuffled into the kitchen. "Anyone want some coffee, tea?"

Isaiah narrowed his eyes at the fellas and quietly stated, "It's late and Mama's tired, whether she admits it or not. She needs her rest. You got me?" All six eyes shifted to each other to gauge their response. Once they reached a nonverbal understanding, the men strolled toward the kitchen door.

Benjamin spoke up first. "Well, Mae."

"It's Hattie," Clarence corrected him. Isaiah rolled his eyes. Nobody else paid him a bit of attention.

"I'm gonna get on outta here. You call me if you need anything."

"Or me."

"Anything at all. No matter the time."

Isaiah cut in. "I'll be here with her. She'll be just fine."

"That's right. She'll be in excellent hands with my son." Benjamin smiled like a proud parent. Isaiah's eyes rolled so hard he looked like he was in pain. Benjamin planted a big kiss on Hattie's cheek, and they hugged. Clarence watched and counted how long their embrace lasted. When he got to four, he got hot.

"All right, all right, all right. Break it up. Let the lady breathe." Benjamin stared Clarence down as he wiggled his body between them. The move left Hattie both appalled and amused until Clarence slightly dipped her for a kiss.

"Get yo greasy lips off of her," hollered Benjamin. The men pushed each other, leaving Isaiah no choice but to step in once again; this time, he booted both from the house.

"I'm sick of these grown-ass men acting like kids, and I have to be the damn referee," Isaiah spat. He looked over at his mother and left the kitchen, disgusted. Hattie sipped her tea with a smile.

*   *   *

"Clarence, I told you, I just don't know." Hattie's voice was getting stronger and stronger by the day, and she knew she would definitely attract a crowd. Isaiah stood over her, lips too tight to sip water—something she'd grown accustomed to, especially since she began dating Clarence. "Now I don't want to talk about this anymore until I bring it up again, hear?" Hattie quietly hung up the phone and picked up her newspaper without looking up at Isaiah. She was in no mood.

"He still pressuring you to marry him?"

"Yes."

"You gonna keep draggin' this out or what?"

Hattie huffed. "Whatchu talkin 'bout, boy?"

"You know what I mean." He plopped down on the sofa across from her.

Damn. He just had to get comfortable.

"If you wanted to marry him, you would've said so by now. It's been what, almost a year?"

"It has not been a year."

"Yeah, it has," Christopher jumped in on the conversation.

"Boy, where'd you come from? Don't you eva scare me like that." Hattie said while holding her chest.

Isaiah rushed over to her. "You okay, Mama?"

"Yeah, he just scared the devil out of me! Now stay outta my business."

"We just want you to get real about what you want," Isaiah said.

Hattie looked over her glasses. "When have you ever known me to not be real?"

"She's got a point there, bruh." Both Hattie and Isaiah looked at Christopher until he backed up and left the room.

"I know you can look out for yourself, but what kind of son would I be if I didn't protect you, Mama? Let me do my job."

Hattie sighed. "I know, I know."

"And both of these fools gotta go."

"Both of them?"

"Yes, they are clowns, Mama. You deserve better, don't ya think?" Hattie got up and left the room. "Mama?"

"Yes, baby?"

"I didn't hear your answer."

"I missed your question. Say it one mo' time." Hattie shuffled into the kitchen and banged almost every pot and pan together on the counter. Isaiah followed her.

"Boy, you love the attention from Frick and Frack, don't you?" Hattie couldn't look Isaiah in the eye and followed up with some stuttering. He grabbed a peach, excused himself, and went to bed. He was through arguing for the night.

The next morning, Hattie woke up sweating. She sat up in the bed, huffing and puffing. She'd had a nightmare. This one seemed so real. Hattie was in a dark basement with the walls closing in on her. She couldn't move other than her head. Hattie screamed, but no one came. She was alone and frightened. She recognized this dream. Hattie'd had it at least once a month for the last seven months, but it hit differently this day. A knock at the door brought her back to reality. "Who is it?"

"It's me, Mama. Can I come in?"

"Come on." Isaiah tiptoed in. Hattie grabbed the hand towel she kept by her bed and wiped her face.

"Having that dream again, huh?"

"Yup. Actually, I'm glad you came in here."

"What's going on?" He sat next to her on the bed.

Hattie let out a deep sigh. "I'ma need you to stay here with me, all right?"

"Another night? Sure, until you fall asleep."

"Now you know damn well that's not what I said."

"No," Isaiah said flatly. He stood to leave.

"Hear me out."

Now it was Isaiah's turn to sigh heavy. "This oughta be good." He sat back down and looked down at his feet. She waited until he looked at her.

"I'm getting a little up there, and before you know it, I won't be able to take care of myself no more."

"As much as you've sweetened the pot, I'm not gonna have you in here not being able to do for yourself."

"That's part of it. I don't need you swooping in here to take care of me when I'm all spooky in the head."

"Spooky in the what?"

"You know what I'm tryna say. Don't wait till I can't do for myself and then come up in here and try to take over. I want you here now so you can keep me motivated and moving."

"Mama," Isaiah looked at her and snickered. "You can get a life coach or what have you."

"What I want with that? Sounds expensive." Hattie rolled her eyes. "Just keep an open mind, all right?"

"Fine." Isaiah stood and kissed her on her head.

"So, you'll think about it?"

"Nope."

Hattie threw the closest thing to her. Her damp towel popped Isaiah in the butt.

By the time Hattie reached the kitchen, Isaiah had a plate ready for her. The scrambled eggs, hash, toast, and orange slices looked almost as good as her own cooking. She bent his head to kiss his forehead.

"You're welcome, Mama." Isaiah smiled. A playback of their conversation earlier clouded his head. *Is she hiding something from me? Whatever it is, I'm sure I'll have to drag it out of her.* "When's your next doctor appointment?"

"Today."

He slammed the fridge. "Ah, Mama! Why didn't you tell me?"

Hattie took a bite out of her toast and crunched. "You didn't ask. And by the way, don't slam my door. You know better than that."

They met eyes, one set full of fury and the other indifferent. "Again, why didn't you tell me? You know I would like to be there."

"Well, all right. You can take me."

"How were you planning on gettin' there? Your old man?"

"Nah, I didn't want him in my business like that. 'Sides, I told him you were going to take me."

"You make absolutely no sense right now. You told him about your appointment, didn't tell me, but expect me to take you. You know what, never mind." Isaiah stopped.

"I was about to ask you why you're getting so excited. Raising my pressure just looking at you," Hattie remarked, sipping some tea.

"When is it?"

"'Leven." He glanced over at the clock. In angry letters, it read 9:30. He closed his eyes and counted to himself before he blew a gasket. Hattie never took less than an hour to get ready. Isaiah took monstrous steps toward the family room and sat fuming.

When Hattie returned to the kitchen, Isaiah was hunched over a chair, staring at the ground. "You all right?"

"Yup."

"I think we're running a little behind, so you'll need to take the molasses out of your foot and step on it." She grabbed a fistful of chips out of a bag. He snatched the bag from her and threw them on the counter.

"I'm not gonna speed because you took too long in the bathroom. I already called. Let's go." Isaiah opened the door for his mother and rolled his eyes after she passed. He was angry, not foolish.

Dr. Heath always had a packed schedule, but he took his time with Hattie, partly because she didn't like to be rushed and because he needed enough time to coax the truth out of her. He had been Hattie's doctor ever since she'd moved to Michigan. So, he knew when she was telling him what he wanted to hear.

After a loud knock, the door swung open. "Ms. Atkins, wonderful to see you! How's it going, Isaiah?" Dr. Heath and Isaiah's hands met firmly.

"Could be better."

"Oh yeah?" Hattie might not have caught on, but Dr. Heath always asked this of Isaiah first to get a read on her. A response like this often meant the visit would lead to her cussing, fussing, and shutting down. Doc knew he had to tread lightly. "How are you feeling, Ms. Atkins? Are you following that diet I suggested?"

Isaiah's snicker was met with a nasty stank eye. "Is your name Ms. Atkins? Is there something *you* gotta tell me?" Isaiah moved to the furthest corner of the room and sat stone-faced. "I'm doing all right, doc. I fell off a couple of days with the diet, though." Hattie ignored Isaiah's next snicker. "I don't think it's right for me."

"Well, you don't want to end up in the hospital again, do you? I want to make sure you're taking good care of yourself, all right?"

"I hear what you're saying, doc, but a cup of this and a cup of that does nothin' for me. I need all my starches and a big-ass piece of pie when I'm through. You hear me?"

Isaiah rested his face in his palms. *Damn, she's stubborn!*

"As tempting as that sounds, pie after almost every meal is just too much. Moderation—remember we talked about that? I'm not trying to cut everything out of your diet, just right-sizing it, all right? So, let's check you out."

Dr. Heath checked her vitals and had her describe how she'd been doing, what exactly she'd been eating, and what exercises she'd been doing within the last three weeks. Isaiah laughed when she counted wobbling up and down the stairs to answer the door as part of her exercise regimen. He explained to Isaiah that it would take baby steps to get exercise on her schedule since she wasn't used to it. "Be careful on those steps. I don't want you to get hurt. Also, there are some things you can do while sitting." Once Dr. Heath showed her some exercises, he let her go with a semi-stern warning to do something quick, or he'd have to see her more frequently or in the hospital.

The ride home was quiet until they turned into the neighborhood. "Look at all these damn kids with their toys all spread out over the yard. And look at this one riding his bike in the middle of the street, begging to get hit."

"At least they're exercising."

"Oh, shut up."

"Mama, I really wish you'd take this more seriously. I'm really starting to think you're not taking care of yourself to make me move back home, but I can't. I have my own family now, and I need you to do for yourself. Stick around for a bit, you know?" His lecture was interrupted by his cell. Lucky for him, because Hattie was gearing up to cut loose. Raine needed him. "We'll have to finish this later—or actually, I'd rather not."

Isaiah pulled into the driveway and both removed their seatbelts. "No, don't. I got it from here. I don't want to burden you with helping me in the house." Before Isaiah could argue, a black Cadillac slowly pulled in behind Isaiah.

Hattie waved Clarence away, but he didn't get it, so she waited until he climbed out. "Move out the way, you ole fool. The boy gotta leave." Clarence hopped back in and crept out of the driveway to the front of the house. By the time he parked, Hattie was inside brewing some tea.

Clarence slithered in and removed his hat. "Hey, Suga! What'd the doctor say?"

"Nothing much. I just have to move a little more, that's all."

"Well, we can make that happen." Clarence puckered up but was left hanging. The phone rang; Hattie went to the family room to grab it.

"Hello?"

"How ya feeling, Mama?" Benjamin's deep voice sent a tingle down her spine.

Hattie smiled. "I'm hanging in there. Whatchu up to?" She didn't realize her shadow was behind her.

"Who is … that better not be Casper!"

She jumped and covered the receiver. "Stop with all that hoopin' and hollerin' in my house."

"I'm not yelling at you. I want *him* to hear me."

"Everybody in Oakland County can hear you. Just hush."

Benjamin sighed. "You gonna marry that ole goat?"

"I don't want to talk about that right now." Clarence plopped on the sofa across from Hattie and watched every word. "Get out of my mouth, Clarence! You know what, I gotta go. I'll talk to you later."

"Later? As in tonight?" Clarence slid to the edge of his seat.

"Clarence!" Hattie slammed down the phone and hopped out of the chair. Her quickness surprised them both. She pointed her finger in his face. "I don't need you in my business."

"You are my business, lady."

"You are *just* my boyfriend, and that can definitely change."

Ignoring Hattie in his face, he replied. "I don't want you as my girlfriend, I want you as my wife. So, what's it gonna be? I'm tired of waiting—"

"I'm tired too, Clarence."

Her tone caught him off guard and on edge. "So, what does that mean?"

Hattie took a step back and looked Clarence in the eye. "I think we're done here."

"Huh? Suga, whatchu saying?" He stood.

"Get out of my house, Clarence. I can't do this with you no mo'."

He reached for her, and she stepped back. "Baby, let's talk about it for a minute. Don't make any rash decisions when your sugar's low. I can't leave like this. Let's talk about it when I get back home tonight and you've had some time to think. Come on, now."

Hattie turned and headed upstairs. "Lock that door behind you."

Clarence grabbed his hat on the way out and locked the door as requested. *I'll wait until she cools off a lil bit. I know she didn't mean this is over.*

Hattie listened for the door closing and Clarence's car driving away before she let the tears flow. Clarence meant well, but there was no way she could marry a man like that. So insecure, childish, and jealous. She'd rather be alone.

She'd thought a lot about remarrying, especially after her hospital stay. But more importantly, Hattie considered Benjamin as an option, and that scared her. With him calling her daily to check on her, she let her guard down a lot more than expected. Had he really changed like he claimed? Was he talking to his ex-fiancée or any other women? Why did he *really* come back into her life? The confusion with Benjamin, for some reason, made him more desirable. *Now how does that work?*

Hattie gave herself ten minutes to get herself together before she called Benjamin back, but she made another call first. On the third ring, she got a reply. "It's over."

"What is?"

"Me and Clarence."

Isaiah sat up on the couch. "Are you serious?"

"Yes."

"Thank God."

"Just wanted you to know. Enjoy your evening." She could hear Raine's voice and the TV playing softly in the background. She didn't want to say too much until she cleared her head more; then they could talk privately. Plus, Hattie didn't want to take any more of Isaiah's time away from Raine. Last, but certainly not least, her final call.

"Hey, back so soon?"

"Do you still love her?"

"What?" Benjamin questioned. Hattie felt he paused too long.

"Welp, got my answer. We'll talk another time." Hattie hung up and went to bed by 5 p.m., which she only did when she was sick. She needed some sleep and alone time, no foolishness. Her phone rang several times throughout the night from all her men—Clarence, Isaiah, and Benjamin. It was nice to be wanted, but she was exhausted.

* * *

Two weeks later, her bestie, Sis Bea, picked Hattie up to attend Bible study. She hadn't gone since her surgery and was feeling disconnected from her church. Pastor Stanley had stopped by and called a couple of times since then, but it wasn't the same. She needed to see her people and worship alongside them.

It was a lot better than sulking around thinking about the two stooges. The last thing she wanted to see or hear about was a ring. Hattie Mae Atkins would not be pressured into marriage from Mo or Curly!

As they entered the church, a small crowd gathered around Hattie, and everyone was talking at once. *How have you been? Are you taking it easy? Who's helping you around the house? You look good. You lost a bit of weight, didn't you?* It wasn't until she was among her friends that she realized how much she'd missed them.

Pastor Stanley called the class to order, and the room silenced. "Good afternoon, everyone. It's so nice to see all of you. Thank you for coming out to worship. Today we have a very special guest who comes to us looking nice and healthy, and we thank God she is still with us. Can we take a second to give Ms. Hattie Mae Atkins a hand praise?"

The class gave her a standing ovation, as Hattie stood and hugged Pastor Stanley. She wasn't expecting all this attention, but she wasn't going to let it go to waste. "Thank you, everyone. Like Pastor said, I'm so happy to be here with y'all, and of course, above ground." The class laughed. "I'ma stop taking things for granted, and people too. I'm ready to see the King, but not just yet."

Everyone laughed, but not Hattie. She was serious and wanted everyone to know there were going to be some changes coming. She would hold some closer, and others she would boot from her life. When she was in the hospital, she noticed who was by her side and who was silent. Those who checked on her, called, and visited her, she'd make sure she was fully present with them. That was the least she could do. Hattie peered at everyone. Some smiled and others squirmed in their seats. *Yup, Mama's nice list will be cut a lil short.*

After Bible study, a smaller crowd formed around Hattie again until Pastor Stanley pulled her away. "Sister Hattie, can I have a moment of your time?" They walked a couple feet away from the cackling women to a quieter spot in the room. His shifty eyes scared her; she'd felt them on her throughout the class. Hattie was unsure if he was talking about her behavior earlier or if he really had something to say. "Sister, I usually don't do this, but would you like to have dinner with me Sunday evening?"

Hattie rapidly blinked. The last thing she thought about was Pastor having a crush on her. Her stomach fluttered. *I wonder how long Pastor has been feeling this way. What happened to Sister Evelyn? That*

You Never Know | 125

would make me a cougar, but I'm okay with that. Does this mean I could possibly become a preacher's wife and closer to Jesus? She straightened her back, patted her stringy wig, and batted her eyes. "That would be delightful." *Delightful? I've never used that word my whole entire life! Keep it cool.*

Pastor shifted. "Great! I live right behind the church." He grabbed a scrap sheet of paper and jotted down his address. "See you soon, Sister."

Hattie beamed as she watched him walk away. She never thought of him as more than a pastor, but she'd definitely think about it now.

Sis Bea had quietly observed their interaction. "Whatchu got going on, Hattie?"

"Oh! You scared the devil outta me!" Hattie spat while catching her breath. "Stop creepin' up on me, Bea. You ready to go?"

"I'm ready when you are."

The two women waved and hugged goodbye to everyone, then headed to the car. Once they exited the church, Sis Bea started up again. "I know my cataracts usually be actin' up, but I know I saw you and Pastor getting a little more, how would you say it, acquainted. Giggling and whispering all in each other's faces."

"Yo blind ass didn't see a thing."

Sis Bea pressed. "I know what I saw. Whether you want to admit to it or not. You've got the hots for Pastor."

"I do not. Just shut yo mouth and drive."

"He's still very married."

"Who you telling? I remember helping Sister Evelyn make some greens a few years ago and she burned the pan before we even got started. She ain't allowed to step foot in my kitchen or the one at the church."

"So then ..."

"No need to strain your wig, Bea. I don't need to narrate my every move to you." They pulled off and rode back to Hattie's in silence. She could tell her friend was hurt by her not spilling the beans, but she felt like keeping a little secret to herself. Plus, there wasn't much to tell, at least for now.

Once in the house, Hattie looked at Pastor's scrap sheet of paper. *Sunday at 5 p.m. 492 Greenlawn St.* Now she needed to occupy her mind for the next two days. Once she changed out of her church clothes, she put on her play clothes: her favorite pink floral muumuu. Next, Hattie did what she did best—cook. This allowed her the peace and space to solve problems, and to talk to herself without disturbing anybody. She had company coming later and wanted to relax before the storm.

Sis Bea was mad at her for not sharing her discussion with Pastor Stanley, but even Hattie was clueless. Sure, they'd had private conversations over the years, but nothing taken off-site or without context. If Pastor had feelings for her, that wasn't her fault. With her recent weight loss, a few men had checked her out here and there, so she wouldn't be surprised either. Hattie smiled at the flattery. She couldn't imagine anything else he couldn't talk about at church. She knew these next couple days were going to be rough waiting, so it was best she occupied her mind.

Hattie took out butter and sugar, and without any recipe in mind, she let her hands guide the rest. After four and a half hours on her feet, Hattie had baked ham, mashed potatoes, corn on the cob, cornbread, mac and cheese, and green beans spread across the table. She sat down in her chair, kicked her feet up, and rested her eyes.

Hattie didn't hear the door open or close. Christopher walked up to the unattended food and quietly sampled each dish. "Damn, grandma! Mm, mm, mm." He rushed over to the sink. If she caught him digging in the food without washing his hands, even while using a fork, he knew there would be dire consequences. He peered over his shoulder and didn't see or hear Hattie. *Just avoided an ass-whupping. Good job, Chris!* Questioning the silence of the house, he walked into the family room to see Hattie stretched out with her eyes closed and mouth open. "Grandma! Grandma!" Christopher violently shook her shoulders.

Hattie's eyes flew open. "What!" She looked up and saw Christopher. "Boy, get your hands off me. Are you crazy?"

"I thought you were dead."

"I don't die every time I close my eyes. Ever heard of a nap?" She moved to the edge of her seat. "You keep scaring the shit out of me like that and you will kill me!" She struggled to get to her feet, shooing his help away. "You been in my food?" Hattie squinted her eyes at him.

"I just took a little piece."

"Bet your hands weren't even clean. Now the food's contaminated."

"Aw, grandma. My hands are clean. See, smell them."

"Get out the way, boy." Christopher followed her to the kitchen. "Where's grandma's baby?"

"Lesha will be in with him in a second. She was waking him up," Christopher explained.

"Someone else you won't let sleep. Now we'll both be cranky."

Lesha strolled in with CJ. "Hey, Ms. Atkins. How are you feeling?"

"Still above ground. There's grandma's baby! Y'all go wash your hands and make your plates. Everybody should be here in a minute. Christopher, take that pie out the oven. I got him." Hattie grabbed the baby carrier and plopped down in a seat to hold her grandson. Hattie and Christopher decided not to make things complicated—he was her grandson, and she was CJ's grammy. It wouldn't make sense for CJ to call Benjamin "grandpa" and her "great grammy."

"You not gonna eat?" Christopher asked.

"I will in a minute." Hattie freed CJ; Christopher watched her eyes dance for his son. He had never witnessed this kind of joy. He wished his parents made him feel this type of love. Christopher was sure his mom loved him, but at the same time, he hadn't seen or heard from her in years, or anyone else on her side. He mainly spoke with his dad when they'd run into each other at Hattie's or special events, and he was fine with that. Although Hattie fussed at him all the time, he knew she loved him as her own. That was good enough for him. "Don't forget the pie."

Christopher sprang into action. "Oh, let me wash my hands again."

"Yeah, I bet," Hattie said snidely.

After a few minutes, the phone rang; Christopher answered and handed it to Hattie.

"Hello?" Hattie scowled when she heard Benjamin's voice. She wasn't ready to speak with him yet, but here he was. *He wasn't this consistent when we were married.*

"I was hoping I'd catch you alone. There's something I need to talk to you about, face to face. So I'm headed into town tomorrow night."

"What is so important that you have to drop everything and come all the way up here in my face?" Something else Hattie didn't know how to handle and didn't want to deal with right now. She was struggling to identify what feelings she was having for Benjamin. The love for him never went away, but she was confused if she was back *in* love with him. Seeing him again without that clarity now, being newly single, might take her further down the rabbit hole. Hattie was too busy listening to what was going on outside as another car pulled in and two doors slammed. She totally missed how Wild Cat answered, and instead of asking him to repeat, she quickly dismissed him and hung up.

"What's going on, y'all?" Isaiah hugged Christopher and Lesha, then headed into the family room. "Hey Mama."

He leaned down to kiss his mother and nephew; Raine stepped into the room and doled out hugs and kisses.

The family sat down to eat together. Without Clarence and Benjamin there bickering and trying to one-up each other, it was the loving atmosphere they all needed. This was the one thing Hattie always wanted—all her family together at the table; talking, laughing, and breaking bread. Lisa was the only missing piece, plus her family that Hattie really hadn't gotten to know yet. She was still heavily living with regret on her decision to kick her out of her house, and she was dealing with those consequences, but not well. Lisa had started calling Hattie at least once a week since her party, which increased to two to three times since her heart attack. Hattie often prayed for the day her whole family would live in the same city, so this kind of fellowship would come naturally instead of planned.

"Anybody got any plans this weekend?" Isaiah asked. "Raine is dragging me to some shopping outlet tomorrow." The family laughed.

"We need some new stuff—furniture, clothes, everything! Don't act like you're not excited," said Raine.

"All I hear is, *money, money, money.*"

Raine rolled her eyes.

"You must've bribed him to go. He hates shopping." Christopher added.

"Tell me about it!" Raine laughed.

"Well, I'm going to have dinner with Pastor." The room went silent, except for Christopher dropping his fork.

Isaiah spoke first. "You mean with Pastor Stanley and the First Lady."

"Um, I don't think so. He asked me to have dinner with him, and I said yes."

"I don't get it. What's happening here?" Isaiah prodded.

"It's just food, damn! Trying to get into Heaven, so I'm not gonna mess that up for nobody." Hattie sucked her teeth. The men exchanged disapproving glances and the women looked down at their food. They all knew there was no convincing her to decline the suspicious invitation.

"Well, I've got some news. We 'bout to have another baby," Christopher exclaimed.

The beaming couple was met with hugs and congratulatory messages, except Hattie. "You just dropped this one. You couldn't wait a minute?"

"Grandma, it wasn't planned, but I mean …" Christopher's voice trailed off.

"Still ain't using my baby shower gift, huh," Hattie sucked her teeth.

Christopher snickered. "How long do you think a pack of condoms 'posed to last?"

Raine jumped in. "We are so happy for you and Lesha. Do you know what you're having yet?"

She grinned, happy to be invited into the conversation. "Not yet. We find out in a couple weeks."

"Wonderful. We can't wait to meet the newest little Atkins," said Raine.

"You can barely afford this one. How—"

"Mama, let it go," Isaiah cut in. He wanted her to be happy and to stop controlling everyone. He'd witnessed the pain and guilt she wore for the last few decades since her blow-up with his sister. Isaiah couldn't stand the thought of being around for another.

"Fine." Hattie wiped her mouth and threw her napkin on the table. "I'm sure y'all can take care of all this. I'm going to bed." She stubbornly left the room despite her family's protests. Isaiah wanted to follow her, but knew it wasn't wise.

The family finished their food and quietly cleaned up the kitchen and dining room. They softly debated who should go talk to Hattie. Lesha decided it would be her.

Christopher's eyes widened. "Baby, I think you should slow down about going up there."

"What do you think she's going to do, throw me down the stairs?" she joked. Lesha's smile faded when she was the only one laughing. "I will be fine."

"If you insist. I'll be right outside the door."

Lesha gingerly climbed the stairs as Christopher crept behind her. Not sure what she was going to say, but hoping Hattie would give her a chance, she lightly knocked on the door. "Ms. Atkins? This is Lesha, may I come in?" After almost an excruciating minute, Hattie told her to come in. She tiptoed into the dimly lit room and closed the door behind her. "Thank you for letting me in."

Hattie wasn't in bed yet, just sitting on the edge with her table lamp on, in her nightgown, with the sheets pulled back. "What can I do for you?"

"I know this baby was a surprise—"

"Like the other one?"

"Yes, but he or she will still be loved. We're far from rich, but we'll continue to work hard to make sure they're both taken good care of. Isn't that what's most important?"

Hattie sighed. "I don't want y'all struggling the way I did. And when Lisa got pregnant after watching me struggle—I just can't." Her disappointment left her tongue-tied, which frustrated her.

"We'll be okay, and we're not going anywhere." Lesha attempted to sit next to Hattie, but was met with questioning eyes.

"Where you going with your street clothes still on?"

"Oh." She straightened herself up.

"Christopher, get in here." The door cautiously opened.

"How you know I was up here?"

Hattie pursed her lips and continued. "I'm okay, just needed a minute. I'm not gonna push away any more family that I love. Y'all hard-headed; hormones raging. Just wish y'all would slow down and enjoy life for a while when you're still young. I'ma still love this knucklehead like the first one." Christopher hugged her tight and Lesha joined. She tried to fight it, but ultimately put her arms around both.

* * *

The last two days were some of the longest Hattie had ever spent waiting for anything. She tried to keep her mind occupied, but everyone around her kept reminding her about her date. She was so annoyed with Sis Bea, she skipped service for fear she would cuss her out again. Bea called her before and after church and was met with only her voicemail.

Once 3 p.m. hit, Hattie started getting ready for the big dinner. She took her time. Hattie wasn't sure what to expect, but made sure to apply perfume to her cleavage and behind her ears. She wore her white gloves; the same gloves she used to wear when ushering. She pulled her hair back into a bun and had the audacity to put on some lipstick she didn't realize she still had. Now fully dressed, she went downstairs and was met with Isaiah's disapproving stare.

"There's still time to not go."

"Oh hush and button me up."

Isaiah reluctantly unfolded his arms to button the back of her dress. He also had a choice: take his mama to Pastor's house or take her to get something to eat himself. He knew she hadn't eaten much all day and worried about her health—no less than what this secret meeting was about.

They climbed into the car. Hattie hummed most of the way while staring out into space. Isaiah wondered what she was thinking, but knew she wouldn't share any details, if anything at all. A short twenty minutes later, Isaiah pulled into the driveway. "Still time."

"Get yo ass out the car and help me."

Isaiah helped Hattie out of the car. She fussed when he tried to walk her to the door. She didn't want Pastor Stanley to think she needed assistance. Isaiah backed off, but waited by the car. Hattie rang the bell and Pastor greeted her with a smile.

"Right on time! Good to see you, Sister Hattie."

"You may call me Hattie or just Mae, Pastor."

"Yes, ma'am, Ms. Hattie Mae. Good to see you too, Isaiah!" He didn't feel right only using her first name. He wasn't raised that way.

Why can't I come in and eat? What's the big deal? Isaiah threw a quick wave and got into the car. He wasn't going to go far; he wanted to stay close in case Pastor got fresh. It would've been different if they'd met at church, but something didn't sit right with this super private event. Isaiah decided to grab a quick bite, then go back and park out front.

Pastor helped Hattie into the house. The smell of spaghetti sauce filled her nostrils. "Mmm, spaghetti?" Pastor nodded. "Oh boy. Who made it?" Hattie stopped in her tracks. *Let Pastor say Sister Evelyn made this shit and I'm out.*

"I did."

Hattie blurted out, "Good. A man that cooks—definitely sweetens the pot."

"What was that?"

"Smells good enough to eat out the pot." Hattie winced, hoping Pastor Stanley really didn't hear her original thoughts. They walked into the dining room after making a pit stop to wash her hands. Just as Hattie took her place at the dinner table and complimented the décor, they had company.

"Hi there, Sister Hattie. Glad you could make it." Sister Evelyn came in with their six-week-old on her hip and gave Hattie a sideways hug.

What the hell is going on here? "You know I don't usually pass up a good meal with good *people*." Hattie sarcastically chuckled. She stretched her neck. "Anyone else coming?"

"No, it's just us." She smiled, took her seat, and placed the baby in a highchair. "Michael is at a friend's house."

"She's adorable."

"Thank you," Sister Evelyn said.

"She's actually the reason we've called this gathering." Pastor took his seat at the head and continued. "Well, maybe we should eat first before diving right in." He smiled sheepishly.

"We can't do both?" Hattie challenged.

Sister Evelyn bumped the table getting up and quickly slapped salad, spaghetti, and bread on their plates. Pastor waited until she finished serving before continuing. "Well, Ms. Mae."

"Sister Hattie."

Pastor was taken aback by her reversal. "Sister Hattie, you know we both adore you. We see you in church every Sunday, so we know you have a good Christian heart of gold. Not only that, we've gotten a chance to get to know you over the last I don't know how many years and we think of you as family. So, it's only fitting that we ask—"

The doorbell rang, followed by a heavy knock. All exchanged curious looks until Pastor Stanley left the table to answer the door. "Hey, what's up?"

Hattie heard mumbling, but couldn't make anything out. When she looked up, she almost gagged on a meatball. Pastor entered the room with Isaiah. His eyes met his mother's irritated eyes.

Hattie dabbed her mouth and rested her arms on the table with a thud. Isaiah stared blankly at her, then tried to hide a smile.

"Whatchu doing in here? We've barely even started eating yet."

"Sorry to interrupt your lil date, but I brought your phone. You left it in the car."

"My phone?"

"Date?" Pastor questioned. "Oh no, we just wanted to ask a big favor and wanted to do it while having dinner. That's all."

"I guess you can say a family dinner date," Sister Evelyn said to Isaiah.

He looked over at Sister Evelyn and nodded hello; it was the first he'd noticed her. *Now I feel better.*

"Oh, my fault."

"Boy, you know it wasn't that serious. I don't even use that ole thing."

"I mean, you never know," Isaiah weakly countered.

"Nosy," Hattie mumbled and sucked her teeth.

"Why don't you join us, Brother Isaiah?" Sister Evelyn cut in.

"Well, I don't want to impose."

"Then don't. Come back in 30." Hattie spat and then turned to Pastor. "So, what's the favor?"

Isaiah had no problem leaving. His belly was full anyway. He was just relieved he didn't walk in on some funny business. Isaiah was now fully comfortable leaving her there by herself.

"Okay, I'll just spit it out. We want you to be Sarah's godmother," Pastor said. Hattie's mouth dropped. He quickly added, "Several of our family members are either deceased or not quote unquote stable enough for the task, but you're perfect. Even though you recently had a setback, you're a God-fearing woman, a mother and grandmother, protective, and you love children. We want you to bless her with your presence, family, and many gifts."

Hattie's eyes softened. "Nobody has ever asked me to do that. What all do I need to do?"

Sister Evelyn chimed in. "Just be there for Sarah, especially after our passing."

"Y'all *both* 'bout to die?" Hattie questioned.

Pastor chuckled. "No, but we're at the point in our lives where we're putting our affairs in order. It's a lot to think about, but we want you to truly consider it. We also wanted to give you the opportunity to consider it privately, instead of in front of everybody at the church."

"I appreciate being thought of in this way. What about Michael? His Godmother too?"

"No, we've got him covered and don't want to switch things up."

"Mkay, I'll let you know what I come up with." The couple exchanged glances, unsure what Hattie meant. They decided to eat before the food got cold.

Pastor, Hattie, and Sister Evelyn finished their meals and ended up thoroughly enjoying themselves. To Hattie, it felt freeing to get out of the house for a while, taking a night off from cooking and sharing a meal with another family—her extended family.

When Hattie and Isaiah got home, they noticed a car in the driveway. Once Isaiah parked, Benjamin hopped out of the car to meet his family at the door.

"What's up, man? Back again?"

"How ya doing, Isaiah. Just trying to talk to Mae about something important."

"So what's going on?" Hattie asked.

"Can we talk inside?" Isaiah stepped next to Hattie. "Alone," Benjamin added.

"Come on." Hattie went in first, dropped her purse and keys off on the kitchen counter, and gestured to Benjamin to join her at the table. Isaiah kept walking into the family room and turned on the TV—low.

Benjamin, seated across from Hattie, took her hand and looked her in her eyes. "Before I start, everything okay?"

"Whatchu mean?"

"Everything good with your doctor appointment and the breakup?"

"I'm doing just fine."

"So, does that mean that 'Three Piece' is gone for good?"

"Three Piece?"

"Every time I saw the ole goat, he had a three-piece suit on."

"Benjamin, get to the point." He clenched his teeth. Hattie rolled her eyes, but wanted to laugh so bad. She was not in the mood for jokes or jealous rants. "Just got back from Pastor's house. They want me to be their baby's godmother. I'm on a high right now and don't need no more foolishness."

He stretched his eyes. "What? Are you serious? What made them choose you?"

"Whatchu tryna say?" Hattie jumped out of her seat. "I'm not good enough to be a Godmama?"

Benjamin stood. "I'm not saying that at all. Y'all not family, so I was just wondering why they picked you."

"Said I'm a God-fearing special woman. Any family would be proud to have me! Any other questions?"

"Yeah, would you like to move in with me? We could be one big happy family again." Benjamin flashed a goofy grin. Hattie narrowed her eyes.

"What? You want me to move back down to that hot-ass place—no thank you."

"I'm not talking about 'Sippi." He moved closer to her. "I sold the house. I'm here in Michigan now and I want you to move back in with me."

"Oh, hell naw!" They hadn't seen or heard Isaiah enter the room, but he definitely made his presence known. He stood next to his mother and gently pushed Hattie back in the chair. "Nope. Any more questions?"

A Season

There is a time for everything and a season for every activity under heaven ... a time to love and a time to hate, a time for war and a time for peace. (ECCLESIASTES 3:1-8)

Hattie put her reading glasses on after opening her letter. Usually she threw away unsolicited mail, but this piece sparked her interest, especially since it was from someone in Mississippi. *Someone could've dropped dead or I could've wound up with some money. Who knows.*

Dear Hattie Mae,

I don't know how to tell you this so I'll come right out and say it. I'm your sister. I'm not sure what you've heard about me, but I've been in Mississippi all my life and heard you moved away from here some years ago. I'll be visiting Michigan later this month for a week or so and would love to meet you. We have so much to talk about! Write or call me back and let me know when you can meet.

Love, Cora Mae

What the hell is this? "Benjamin, where you get this mess from? Is this a joke?" Hattie flipped both the letter and envelope over looking for anything that indicated a prank.

"It came from your mailbox. What is it?" Benjamin came back into the room and sat across from Hattie. He'd been staying fifteen minutes away from Hattie now for almost six months. Although she appreciated him being there when she needed something fixed or someone to run errands with, she still didn't see the purpose of him giving up his life down south to come be up under her. Hattie figured he felt like he still had a chance with her, even though she was still firmly on the fence about moving forward and his true intentions.

"A letter from somebody's sister. I know I don't have one anymore, so I don't know why this was sent to me."

"Can I see?" Benjamin took the letter from Hattie, slipped his reading glasses on, and read it to himself. "Well, she certainly knows you."

"So did Christopher. 'Memba that?"

"Good point."

"How are these random folks finding me? Just leave me the hell alone."

"Why don't you find out what she's talking 'bout? You don't want to brush her off if she's really your sister."

Hattie peered over her glasses at Benjamin. "Then you go meet her. Let me know how it goes."

Benjamin tsked and rose from his seat. "Sometimes you need to take chances, Hattie Mae. This is family." He left the house.

"Chances, my foot." Hattie mumbled. She read the letter a few more times before throwing it on top of her Bible. She wanted to throw it away but was conflicted. What if somehow she was real, like Benjamin said? She didn't know how it could be possible, but the frustration she felt at not knowing made her even more upset.

The only sibling she knew of was her sister, Lisa Anne, who died from breast cancer over 40 years ago. Now, she did faintly remember her mama losing a child who died at birth. End of story. Roll credits. Unless God was bringing folks back from the grave, she was still good and dead.

On the way to the kitchen, Hattie threw the letter in the trash. This was too much foolishness to deal with; she needed to find something to bake. Hattie left the kitchen at 12:30 a.m. after making apple pie, bundt cake, brownies, and biscuits for the morning.

The next day, Raine stopped by. "Hey, Ms. Mama." When Raine first met Hattie, she called her Ms. Atkins. She called her Ms. for so long, it stuck, and she didn't think Hattie was ready for anyone else to call her Mama, so she combined the two. Hattie liked her special name and appreciated the respect Raine always gave her, which made her love her even more.

Hattie opened the door wide for Raine and they embraced. "How you doing, Suga?"

"I'm wonderful. Just wanted to drop these slippers off for you. How are *you*?" She stepped in and looked around. "Uh oh. I see a dessert buffet. What's going on, Ms. Mama?"

"Oh, nothing."

"Talk to me." Raine sat down at the kitchen table and waited for an explanation. Hattie took a deep breath, then told her about the letter. "Do whatever you think might bring you peace and happiness. If you think meeting her might introduce some trauma in your life, I wouldn't do it right now. You know what I mean?"

"I just wonder why now. What if she, assuming it is my sister, is dying and I don't meet her?"

"How would you feel then?"

"Terrible. Not that I could've done something, but just to see what she's talking 'bout, I guess." Hattie gritted her teeth. "Why the hell did she wait till I'm old as hell to reach out for this nonsense? 'Bout time to lay it down."

"Well, she could've put you on her bucket list."

"Her what?"

"A list of things to do before you die." Raine left the room to wash her hands. When she returned, Hattie sliced a piece of cake for her, wrapping it in a paper towel.

"Baby, sit down and rest your bones. I don't know or care about no list. All I know is, I don't ask for much. Just don't bother me with no silly shit!"

She pinched off a piece of the cake and popped it in her mouth. "Mmm. Thank you, Ms. Mama, but I can't stay. Just stopping by to look at you and drop your shoes off." Any other time, Hattie would've talked her into staying and made her a full plate, but she was stuck in her head. "You already know the answer, and I'm behind you 100% with whatever you want to do." With that, Raine took the rest of her slice, gave Hattie a hug, and left.

Hattie was alone again with her thoughts, which she deemed dangerous. Instead of cooking, she called Sis Bea to take her to church. Sure it was Wednesday, but she knew there was going to be something she could get her hands on or stick her nose in.

An hour later, she was at the other place she called home. Hattie and Sis Bea made a beeline to the kitchen, which was empty, just like the sanctuary and classrooms, until they heard a loud wail. *Finally, sounds of life, even though it sounds like it's dying.* In the last classroom, they peeked and saw Brother Charles sitting behind the piano.

"Oh, I thought I was going to be by myself for a little while longer."

"Didn't mean to scare you, Brother Charles. We were hoping to catch something going on tonight."

"Choir rehearsal will start in about 20 minutes if you care to join, Sisters Hattie and Bea." He gestured toward the empty seats. Both women looked at each other.

"I don't think that was the kind of trouble we were looking for, but thanks though." Sis Bea started to the door, but Hattie caught her.

"Now hol' on a minute, Bea. I've been in almost every committee or group except the choir."

"There's a reason for that, Sister Hattie. Remember?" Sister Caroline strolled into the room and the conversation.

Hattie turned to square off. "Naw, refresh my memory."

Sis Bea swallowed before she continued. "You said you didn't like singing."

"That's a damn lie. Nobody told you that."

"Not in the Lord's house, Sister," Brother Charles reprimanded.

"Excuse me, Brother. But I shouldn't be getting lied on in the Lord's house either."

Sister Caroline cut in. "I can't speak to whether you like to sing or not, but I will say that one day during service we heard you trying to hit high notes from the pew. You sounded like a wolf howling in the wind," Sister Caroline huffed.

"Who died and made you the singing god? At least I don't look like *said* wolf."

Sis Bea snickered. "Oh, grow up, Hattie," Sister Caroline sneered.

"I'm grown. I don't need you or anybody else to tell me what I can't do. Get outta my way!"

Hattie and Sis Bea stayed for rehearsal, and, as Sister Caroline expressed, Hattie howled the loudest. She threw everyone off, which led to the choir being dismissed early. Brother Charles made a mental note to block Hattie from future rehearsals.

Sis Bea dropped an offended Hattie back home and turned in for the night as well. She got to see another side of her friend: tone deaf.

Two weeks later, after Sis Bea made several attempts to talk to her friend, Hattie finally answered her call like nothing happened, and after church, the two left for the grocery store. Hattie had forgotten to make rolls for Sunday dinner, so as much as it pained her, she mentally prepared herself to buy some. She tried to walk past the fresh fruit, but failed once she saw the strawberries on sale. Hattie then had to check out the apples, as she suddenly had a taste for pie. She tossed two off to the side, before fussing out loud.

"Church out already? How'd you get here?" Benjamin startled her.

"Course." She would recognize that voice anywhere, but looked up in time to see he wasn't alone. There was a lady next to him, staring down her throat. "Who's this?"

He blushed, and could've sworn Hattie Mae was a bit jealous of his new lady friend. "Hattie Mae, I'd like you to meet Coral. She's from Jackson, too!" Hattie scrunched her face but remained quiet. Benjamin continued. "We were both grabbing the same pack of chicken in the meat section and just started talking. Ain't that something?"

"You say your name is Hattie Mae from Jackson?" Cora took a step closer.

"It is, and yes."

"Well I'll be! Who would've thought we would reunite in a grocery store!"

"What?" Benjamin questioned. He thought that introducing his new lady friend might spark some interest from his ex-wife, but never considered they would know each other. Then the signature from the bottom of the letter came into focus. *Shit, it's Cora! Thought she said her name was Coral. Probably would not have made the connection anyway. Welp, that adds quite a crinkle*; one he was curious to dabble in.

"It ain't reuniting if we haven't met," Hattie spat. She felt like she was locked in a small closet with no air. Hattie still hadn't decided whether she *wanted* to meet her sister, and this seemed forced. And of all things, she had to be up under Benjamin.

Sis Bea turned the corner and came to a screeching halt when she found her friend. "There you are. Thought you were lost. Hello, Benjamin. Hello." She tilted her head to the stranger, waiting for an introduction, but no one spoke. "I'm Bea, Hattie's closest friend."

Cora stuck out her hand. "Nice to meet you, Bea. My name is Cora. I'm Hattie's sister." Benjamin's eyes closed.

"That's to be determined," Hattie added.

"Oh!" Sis Bea took a step back and looked at her friend. *She never mentioned another sister. What else is she hiding from me?*

"Hattie, this is not how I pictured meeting you either, but we are indeed sisters. I'd like to go somewhere to talk. I'm free most of the week."

"*Cora*, I was married to this woman for over 40 years. You sure you got the right Hattie?"

"Oh please. We've been broken up for at least thirty, thirty-five of them years. Don't forget your infamous disappearing act. And you," she faced Cora, "I have one sister and she's dead. Where the hell you come from, and why now?"

Cora smiled, "You have two."

"Maury says: naw."

"If you want to take a DNA test, that's fine by me. But I'm telling the truth. It took a long time to find you after I found out I wasn't the only child. We both have mama's nose and daddy's beady eyes."

Hattie narrowed her eyes as an arm reached through the small gathering to grab some apples. Hattie huffed, "You know them worms in there will kill you." She wanted to snap the arm in half, but that was the best she could do to contain her anger. Between the customer's rudeness, Cora's persistence, and Benjamin's dumb expression, she couldn't bear to stand there any longer.

"Bea, let's go."

"Did you get the rolls?"

"Heffa, you see any rolls?"

"Hattie Mae, wait! Can we meet for coffee or something? I came all this way."

She turned and stepped inches from Cora's nose. "You didn't come here for me. You were already visiting, but didn't say why. So spill it. Whatchu really here for, huh?"

Cora swallowed. "A procedure. I wanted to meet, just in case."

The only thing missing was a bucket of popcorn for Sis Bea, Benjamin, and the small crowd pretending to shop for apples. Hattie was leery of this, but also wondered if it was true. Was that all Cora wanted from her?

"When's that?"

"Tuesday."

"In two days? Hmph." They looked at each other. "I don't drink coffee, but I can bring some tea by wherever you're staying." Cora beamed as she shared her hotel information and set a time. "Bea, you got this, cause this one don't need to take me to no hotel. I can just hear folks running their mouths."

"Mae, I know you really don't care about what people think about you. 'Cause I have no problems taking you if you need me. Do you need me?" Benjamin asked while inching closer.

"Don't push it. Cora, guess I'll see you tomorrow." Hattie wobbled away and the crowd scattered. She was sure she made the right decision, but also felt she had no choice. *This heffa must be in terrible shape to come all the way here for surgery. At least, she better be after this guilt trip she laid on me!*

The next morning, Hattie's house was quiet enough to hear all the creaks from inside and nature from outside. Animals rustling the leaves, birds singing, and floorboards creaking under her imaginary friend's feet. Sounded like a bootleg symphony. Hattie stomped around the kitchen to add to the racket; mad that the outside carried cheerful sounds, but inside, she was feeling like a stranger in her own house.

How could she be happy with meeting her surviving sister? She didn't understand where she came from. What if she were here to borrow a kidney? Hell, would she even let her? Hattie only agreed to meet to get answers; she looked forward to putting Cora on a plane in a few days.

Sis Bea arrived a few minutes earlier than expected. She knew her friend was already upset and didn't want to push her over the edge. "I brought muffins," she stated as soon as Hattie opened the door. Hattie laughed and it had a domino effect.

"Nobody wants them nasty store brand thangs." Hattie snatched them out of her hands. "I'll nibble, since I didn't make a thing this morning."

"Deal." Sis Bea laid her purse down on the edge of the counter and stared at her friend. "You ready for this?"

Hattie took a small bite, looked at the blueberry muffin, and continued chewing. Unable to tell if she wanted to spit it out or not, she answered while she chewed. "Nope. I wish she'd stop with the mystery shit and just tell me what's wrong with her and what she really wants."

"I know."

"I ain't giving up no kidney for this heffa."

"I know."

"Bea, you gotta throw this shit out."

"I know."

"Tryna kill me. Gonna have me choking on these dry-ass crumbs."

"Let's go, Hattie, and get this over with."

The friends headed to the car and drove the twelve minutes in silence. Even though Hattie didn't like her business being out, she was glad she wasn't alone. With Isaiah and Raine being out of town, there was no one else to go with her and hold her in check. Christopher would only aggravate the situation. When they parked in the hotel's lot a few minutes early, Hattie closed her eyes and hummed Sam Cooke's "A Change is Gonna Come."

"I was born—"

"No, Hattie."

"No?"

Sis Bea shook her head. She'd heard enough of Hattie's caterwauling to know that she didn't need to revisit her sour notes. "Let's just go inside."

Hattie's usual hardened face appeared sullen and pale. Once they entered the hotel lobby, she found a sofa to plop down on. Sis Bea sat next to her, with her head on a swivel. She didn't want to miss a thing; meanwhile, Hattie didn't want to miss another breath. All the excitement leading up to this moment had drained her and left her ready to hop back in bed, and it was not quite 9:30 a.m.

One minute passed; "Welp, she ain't as punctual as me." Sis Bea rolled her eyes.

A few minutes later, Cora stepped off the elevator and headed straight toward the ladies. "Well, good morning," her guests spoke.

"Would you care to grab a cup of coffee from the cafe, or tea, I mean?" She looked at Hattie.

"Naw, I'm good."

Cora looked around nervously, then took a seat on the edge of the armchair across from them. She swallowed and looked around. "I'm so glad you came today." She cleared her throat and appeared to be stuck.

Hattie followed her eyes to the elevator and saw Benjamin step off. He paused, unsure how to play it. "Hey, Hattie Mae. Boy, they have the best coffee cake—"

Hattie stood and shouted. "You slept with my sister?" Other guests and staff froze. Benjamin continued making his way over to the group. He fingered the hem of his shirt.

"Mae."

"Yes or no? And you know damn well ain't no coffee cake served upstairs. How could you sleep with her after you *knew* she was my sister?" He reached for her, but she backed away. She sneered at Cora. "So you came to just meddle in my life. That's what this is about? You want what I have?"

"I'm flattered," Benjamin replied. Hattie wanted to slap the smirk off his face.

"Shut up, you ole fool!" She stepped inches away from Cora's face. "You sicken me. Both of you."

Cora took a step back. "Now wait a minute, Hattie."

"Excuse me." A staff clerk approached the group and whispered. "You are more than welcome to step outside to continue your conversation, or lower your voices. The guests are disturbed."

"I don't give a damn." Hattie sucked her teeth.

"We'll be sure to keep our voices down." Benjamin looked to Hattie. She huffed. The staff clerk eased away, not sure if there would be any more problems, but not quite wanting to stick around to find out.

Cora continued. "What I was going to say is, Hattie, despite all this, I'm so happy to have found you. Yes, I spent a little time with Benjamin, but that's not why I'm here."

"Well, get to it, already."

"Amen!" Sis Bea said in agreement. Everyone forgot she was there. Hattie started to regret the fact that she was. Too much going on for her to know about firsthand.

"Can we please sit?" The group sat. Benjamin attempted to sit next to Hattie, but her stare sent him to the small ottoman. "I'd like to start from the beginning, if I may." Cora ignored Hattie's huff and continued. "From what I was told, Mother gave birth to me—"

"Oh shit. We gotta go back to damn near inception?"

"Hattie, let's give her a chance." Sis Bea was elbows deep in it now.

"—at the hospital. I had some complications, and one of the nurses told her I was dead. That was just a story, obviously. What really happened was that Mother gave birth to me, at the hospital, but she chose not to keep me."

Hattie gasped. "That's a lie!"

"That story about me dying was told over and over, but the truth is, Mother didn't want another mouth to feed or maybe couldn't afford it, so I was left behind. The sweetest nurse, Mary Lee Jones, ended up adopting me. She took care of me from the day I was born till the day she died. God rest her soul. Don't get me wrong, I'm not mad at Mother, I just didn't understand her, that's all. I know she had another baby girl after me, so it didn't make sense."

"I don't understand this at all."

"Well, let me finish." Cora noticed Hattie's shoulders slumping a little, so she knew she was headed in the right direction, but needed her now more than ever. "I was Mama's only child—my mama, not your mama—and I was spoiled rotten! I got a good education, lived in a nice home, and all while living three miles away from you."

"What?" Sis Bea questioned.

"Why didn't you ever say anything?" Hattie asked, not sure whether to stay in shock or to be livid.

"I didn't know! Mama passed last year, and before she died, she sat me down and ran through everything. From family, to bank accounts, to where she wanted to be buried. I needed some time to process everything, and once I did, I started looking for my birth family. I saw where your parents and sister died."

"Lisa Anne," Hattie added.

"Yes. But you were the only one still living. So I tracked you down, and that's when I sent you that letter. Well, after I made sure I was mentally prepared." Cora nervously chuckled.

"So, let me get this straight." Hattie rocked in her seat until she was able to stand up. "Mama left you at the hospital and the nurse took you home. You and your new mama lived a couple of miles away from us, but your mama never said anything about that. You lived a glorious life and now that your mama died, you decided to bust through mine like the Kool-Aid Man. Did I get that right?"

Sis Bea and Benjamin tried to calm Hattie before the storm, but they knew it was too late. And when she erupted, hopefully they'd have enough time to clear out before the cops showed.

"I'm not trying to ruin your life, Hattie. I just want to get to know my sister, that's all. My family. You're all I have left."

"There are ways of doing that other than coming here, saying you're on your deathbed and sleeping with my husband."

"Ex," Sis Bea added.

"I never said I was on my deathbed!"

"Then what's wrong with you and why you need to come all the way up here to get fixed?" Hattie stepped up to Cora. Two staffers stood close on standby.

"Laparoscopy. My doctor, a close friend of mine, recommended one of his former classmates up here. Said she'd take good care of me."

"Lap what?"

"Sounds serious." Sis Bea moved to the edge of her seat.

Cora took a careful seat. "Means they're gonna open up my stomach and look inside. My doctor said there's a growth that needs to be checked out."

"Well damn, I thought you were just fat like me." Hattie took her seat. Her face flushed.

Cora chuckled. "Well, sorta. Is stomach cancer in our family?"

"No, but breast is. That's how I lost mama and Lisa Anne." The group sat in silence for a minute, unsure what Cora would disclose next.

"Why don't you get out of this hotel and stay with me after your lil' thing?" Hattie announced. Sis Bea gasped. "Someone needs to take care of you, right?"

"I wasn't expecting that. You don't have to do that."

"It's settled." Hattie stood. "If you found my address, I'm sure you can find my number to give me all the details about tomorrow. Bea, let's go. I'm beat."

* * *

As requested, Cora called later that night to give Hattie information about her procedure and where to pick her up. They got an opportunity to talk a little more, without an audience, and they both enjoyed it. Hattie hung up the phone after an hour with a smile on her face.

When the doorbell rang, it wiped the smile right off. She shuffled to the door and flung it open. "It's about time you stopped by to see me."

"Hey, Mama. Did you miss me?" Isaiah grinned. They embraced and then sat down to catch up. He detailed his trip with Raine in the Bahamas. Hattie noticed the glowing and relaxed look on his face. She then told him about everything—from the letter, to the supermarket meeting, to Cora's birth story, to Benjamin sneaking off the elevator.

"He was there?"

"That's yo daddy." They both shook their heads.

"I really shouldn't be surprised. That's crazy about Cora. How do you feel about all this? I mean, she did just come outta nowhere. Raine told me that you weren't sure you even wanted to meet her."

"I'm in a better place now."

"Obviously, since you invited her to stay with you. How do you know she really is who she says she is, or what she's really about?" Isaiah asked.

"I tried to pick her story apart, but it makes sense. I remember when I was younger, Mama used to disappear sometimes or take a longer time than usual at the store. I'm *guessing* she knew about Cora and where she ended up. And look at this." Hattie pulled out a charm bracelet she kept in a jewelry box in the next room. "This charm matches the one around her neck. Mama *made* it—one for me and one for Lisa Anne. Tell me that's a coincidence. On top of that, she looks just like Daddy. That's probably why Mama wanted to get rid of her." They shared a laugh.

"I know Granddad was a handful."

"Talks like him too—all slow." They cracked up until tears slid down Hattie's cheeks. She honestly felt good. Did part of her want to take Cora on Maury? Absolutely. But she had been praying about it and knew the Lord wouldn't steer her wrong.

Hattie was in the best place of her life. Her family would all be under one roof soon, with Lisa flying in to meet Cora this weekend. She was back loving the single life. Hattie had her grandson to love on a few times a week and another on the way. She was keeping her weight off by cutting *some* sugar out. For once, in this moment, Hattie Mae Atkins could not complain about anything or anyone, and it tickled her.

Epilogue

Everyone who calls on the name of the Lord will be saved.
(Romans 10:13)

I bet you're wondering what happened to everyone. Well, for starters, Mama has been enjoying babysitting, of all things. Although she fusses about "all these damn kids," she gets awfully irritable when her house is quiet. That includes her goddaughter, Sarah, who has become best buds with Christopher's kids. When she's not entertaining children, she's been dabbling with Wild Cat or another church member named Melvin. Maybe it's the attention, but she loves to see Benjamin pitted against another man. Last year, she and Sis Bea went on a gals' trip to New Orleans. I almost had to go get her! She apparently was partying with some folks *more* than half her age—collecting beads and numbers. As you can see, she's still too much.

Christopher finally saved up to move out of Mama's house for good. He was staying with Lesha and her parents, but once they broke up, he moved into his own place. Christopher enrolled back into community college after he landed a tech job at a Fortune 500 company. He's also been enjoying the single life, but has been mostly focused on co-parenting and providing for his two children. Nia is a feisty five-year-old girl who bats her eyes and gets the world from her daddy, and

CJ has become obsessed with building stuff. We call him Mr. Man, as we can see him putting a roof on someone's house, or building one. Christopher has spoken to his mother once or twice, and during one of those times, he got his aunt's number so they could reconnect.

Lisa visits a few times a year with Simon. Both of their kids have graduated college. Can you believe that? Brandon is a teacher and Gerri started her own fashion line geared toward teens. A few years ago, LeeLee decided to quit her job as bank manager and started her own mental wellness business called Love Like This, which educates the community about mental illness and teaches folks how to love themselves. She credits Gerri for inspiring her to make the leap.

Another source of inspiration for LeeLee's business was Auntie Cora. Yes, she really was Mama's sister—they had their DNA tested. The doctor found a mass and removed it. Although the surgery was a success, staying with Mama didn't help. Mama let her stay for two weeks so she could take care of her and they could get to know each other, but once those two weeks came to a close, we didn't hear from Auntie anymore. They drove each other bananas. Rumor has it, Auntie had some kind of mental health crisis and went downhill from there. She passed away a year ago. Mama still held on to her messing with Benjamin, and snatching some strands of hair from her head (the little she had left) to get it tested also did not help. Needless to say, we did not show our faces at Auntie's service.

Guess I gotta talk about *him*. Benjamin is Benjamin. He's been playing the field, but nothing serious in case Mama ever decides to take him back. He continues to be the apple of LeeLee's eye, and I will say, since he moved closer, we've hung out quite frequently over the last couple of years. Me, him, and Chris have been to games (college and pro), played golf, and overall enjoyed our time together. I never would've thought the day would come when I'd stop being mad at Pops and genuinely love him. It's an awesome feeling and has been an amazing ride.

Almost forgot to update y'all on Clarence the Clown. For the first six months after Mama broke up with him, he continued to call, send flowers, and threaten to visit. Well, one day, he was true to his word and showed up on Mama's doorstep. Unfortunately, that was a day she was feeling "weak" and had Pops over. He answered the door without a shirt on and they finally fought. They tired each other out and Mama never heard from him again. Word is, he met some woman a few weeks later and married her within that year.

And as for me, I've been enjoying married life with my queen. At least once a quarter, we plan a getaway. It helps that Raine's a sought-out motivational speaker. So, I tag along on some of her trips. I'm a few years shy of retirement from my city job, and I can't wait to step away from my desk for good! Whether or not Raine's in town, I still enjoy hanging with Mama, Chris, and Pops for our weekly dinners, but it's even better when the whole gang meets at Mama's.

Children's Books by Kinyel Friday

Believe in Me series

I Am My Hair
Swim Like the Fishes
Not My Lisa

Other Books

I Feel You
Night-Night, Nina

For sneak peeks, bonus content, and more information on upcoming books by Kinyel Friday, sign up for her monthly e-newsletter below.

www.ingramcontent.com/pod-product-compliance
Lightning Source LLC
LaVergne TN
LVHW010217070526
838199LV00062B/4622